KU-439-087

THIS MAN KILLS

A map to the fabled Dutchman Mine — deep in the Thousand Canyons region — inflamed the wild town of Wolflock that Sheriff Craddock thought he'd tamed. Hogan, McCall and Anna Fran believed that the map was the golden key. But they were up against an iron lawman, a killer named Strabo and a host of high-riding hellions. The Wolflock townsfolk believed the chase for the elusive gold was crazy, but for that greedy trio — only hot lead would stop them.

HAMPSHIRE COUNTY LIBRARY	
F	18H617 H35 X
	CO 13905301

BEN NICHOLAS

THIS MAN KILLS

Complete and Unabridged

LINFORD
Leicester

First published in Great Britain in 2005 by
Robert Hale Limited
London

First Linford Edition
published 2006
by arrangement with
Robert Hale Limited
London

The moral right of the author has been asserted

Copyright © 2005 by Ben Nicholas
All rights reserved

British Library CIP Data

Nicholas, Ben
   This man kills.—Large print ed.—
Linford western library
1. Western stories
2. Large type books
I. Title
823.9'2 [F]

ISBN 1–84617–435–X

Published by
F. A. Thorpe (Publishing)
Anstey, Leicestershire

Set by Words & Graphics Ltd.
Anstey, Leicestershire
Printed and bound in Great Britain by
T. J. International Ltd., Padstow, Cornwall

This book is printed on acid-free paper

1

Death of a Badman

'Sorry, honey,' smiled Strabo, reaching for his hat. 'But you know what they say — when you gotta go . . . '

'Just one more drink, Cole?'

She was blonde and beautiful, just the way he liked them. And he'd liked her enough to spend time with her here in her warm, softly lighted cottage on the quiet side of town, well away from Main Street and the bright lights which he must avoid at all costs. But now he really must be riding. A man like Strabo rarely stayed long in the one place, and right now, for desperate reasons of his own, he knew he really shouldn't tarry one minute longer.

Too bad.

For if ever a girl could cause a man to forget his religion or overlook his danger, Anna Fran Hellinger was surely that special one. And, weakening, heard himself say: 'Mebbe just one more.'

So he paused while she poured, and the woman watched him with an all-seeing eye, taking in the whole man at once. She saw the arrogant way he carried his tall frame, the way he had of running fingers carelessly through his mane of glossy black hair. She was also instinctively conscious of his scarcely concealed savagery which he'd tried to hide from her. But what she mostly believed about this one, and the reason behind her invitation to him tonight, was what was being whispered about this badman, namely that he'd been the brains behind the train robbery where innocent men had died and a map of the fabled Lost Dutchman gold mine had been stolen.

Had it not been for his rumoured involvement in that murderous event, Anna Fran would not have given dashing Strabo the time of day much less invited him to her modest home.

For she also wanted to be rich, and maybe was getting just a little desperate.

'Please, handsome, just one more kiss,' she purred. 'You're really something special, you know.'

Sure he knew it. But it was still nice to hear. Yet because he was as tricky as three brush foxes himself, he drew back from her now, quick to scent duplicity or insincerity in others.

'Sorry, honey, but this joker's really got to be riding.' He flashed her that big grin that made him seem handsome even if he really wasn't.

Anna Fran feigned disappointment as she took hold of the flashy red bandanna loosely knotted about his throat.

'I just want you to remember me and promise to stop by and see me again, real soon,' she said, crushing bee-stung lips to his mouth. 'You are the best, handsome — I mean it.'

She didn't mean a word of it, yet for some reason in that special moment the desperado swallowed it whole. As a consequence he felt ten feet tall and bullet-proof without any presentiment of danger as he swaggered down the short dim hallway to the front porch.

He had covered his tracks well, he reassured himself, donning his flash hat and inhaling the clean evening air. Had carefully avoided public places, had even arranged to meet Anna Fran after working hours here, well away from the dangerous front street of one of the toughest towns in the West.

Tonight he brimmed with vigor and assurance as befitted a man destined shortly to become the richest desperado in the Territory. And to sense that he was at last making real headway with the belle of Sunsmoke topped off the biggest week of his life. Why shouldn't he feel ten feet tall on such a Nebraskan night?

He whistled softly as he stepped through the door onto the gallery but stopped abruptly on sighting the big drunk hugging up a roof support just a few feet away.

Strabo's right hand dropped to gun handle and his neck hair bristled with alarm. Then the drunk leaned his head and shoulders over the railing to heave noisily, the bottle in his hand clunking against the railing.

Reassured, the outlaw took his hand off his gun and headed for the steps, thinking magnanimously: *Why should I be the only one havin' a fine old time tonight? To each his own way of funning it up. Go for it, soldier . . .*

It was the hissed intake of a breath behind which alerted him and caused him to whirl just as his boot touched the first step. As he pivoted he threw up his left arm to parry the descending bottle which the fast-lunging 'drunk' was swinging at his head. Panther-quick, his right leg shot out and hooked behind his attacker's rising left knee. Following a lightning pivot to his right, Strabo heaved back with his leg and pushed forward with the entire weight of his body. The big man howled out as he felt his legs torn from beneath him.

His heavy arms flailed in an attempt to save himself and he crashed, heavily and awkwardly down the steps, his head hitting the dry gravel of the yard with a juddering crunch.

One huge leap carried the outlaw clear over the motionless figure to land with catlike agility in the yard, cocked Colt already in hand, every instinct screaming alarm.

Someone was trying to take him alive!

They might well have succeeded had Strabo not made it impossible. The moment he detected movement behind a hedge he cut loose with three rolling shots which came so rapidly they sounded as one. His target figure jack-knifed and hit ground, spewing blood as a stentorian voice rose above the gun echoes;

'Shoot to kill!'

Wild Strabo died as he had lived — outside the law, a pistol in either hand and totally convinced he would survive once more as he'd done so

6

many times before, even as the brutal volleys were slamming his jerking body this way and that under the pitiless moonlight. Until at last he fell with arms wide-flung and face to the night sky as though crucified, finally knowing that this was not just another stinking ambush but the one that counted.

The outlaw died without knowing who had killed him. Only why he had died.

* * *

The sons of a High Plains buffalo hunter and a Fort Lincoln derelict lay sprawled side by side behind the cover of a sunbaked ridge, watching the approaching horseman over their gunsights.

Their sixguns had been dusted with alkali to cut the chance of the metal giving off a warning glitter. Faces and bodies had been similarly camouflaged while they waited motionless towards the end of yet another hot Nebraskan day. They weren't taking any chances today. Gunfighters, opportunists and veterans at all kinds of dangerous work, they were only too well aware of the caliber of the man they meant to capture alive and wheel into town to claim the reward.

'Another fifty yards,' Hogan whispered hoarsely.

'Let him cover another hundred,' argued McCall, anything but calm and confident. 'Damnit, he looks meaner than your girlfriend, Hogan.'

'Who'd you expect a low-down hired killer to look like? Betsy Ross?'

The rider approached, silhouetted against a setting sun. As he drew closer it was seen that he was dressed entirely in black with fancy leather wristlets ornamented with turquoise and silver. His handsome Mexican sombrero sported a wide brocade band from which the brilliant tail-feather of a tropical bird protruded. His weaponry comprised a pair of heavy American Colt revolvers thonged low on supple hips; his eyes were dark and the big Mexican spurs strapped to fancy boots were long and cruel.

The first impression for Hogan and McCall was that if Santa Anna had had more of this breed with him when he crossed the Rio in '36, the war might well have gone the other way.

'Hogan.'

'What?'

'You reckon this is such a great idea?'

'What are you talkin' about? It was your idea, damnit!'

'I thought he was goin' to be some unblown little backshooter, or somethin'. This one looks like you could float a horseshoe in his mornin' coffee.'

'Well, it's too blame late to back off now. Just get ready to take the bastard. Are you ready?'

'Ready as I'll ever be. Go ahead, pard.'

'Reach for the sky, you chilli-eatin' son of a bitch!'

Link Hogan's sudden shout saw the Mexican gunman haul his flashy horse to a dead halt, his startled eyes raking the ridge. The partners were determined to take this man alive or dead, but desperately wished to take him alive. The truth of it was that, despite their renown, they were anything but skilled at bringing home dead meat. But based on the man's appearance and reputation, they fully expected the Rio Kid to slap leather and fight it out to the death, were grimly steadying their gun hands ready to cut him down — when the impossible happened.

The man believed to have been imported specifically to break the deadlock of the Doolin — Caldwell range war with his sixguns jerked his horse and slowly raised kid-gloved hands to shoulder-level.

'Hello?' He sounded nervous. 'Who is it?'

The partners traded an astonished glance. This was a Mexican guntipper imported specifically to tip the scales in a range war?

They jumped up, shedding dust, big

Colts glittering as they strode towards him.

'Get off that nag and get 'em high,' ordered Hogan.

'Like real high — or you're a dead man, killer!' affirmed McCall.

They sounded menacing when really what they mostly were was relieved. Ambush was anything but their speciality, and it had been a bad moment when they realized just how dangerous cattleman Doolin's import appeared at close range. They could scarcely believe their good fortune that he was now acting more like a pushover.

Their man did as ordered. He stood by his mount with an uncertain smile which seemed wildly out of place, considering the circumstances. This was war. They'd been ready to shoot. Didn't he understand this?

'So, what is the problem, *amigos*?' the Chihuahua 'fire-eater' asked as he was relieved of his sixguns. Even his accent sounded bogus, they realized.

'The problem, as you call it, is all

yours, Kid,' McCall said toughly, standing with boots wide-planted and jaw set at an angle, a long-legged Nebraskan sporting two days' stubble. 'We're turnin' you over to Sheriff Craddock, pilgrim, so your part in this war is over before you get to play one card. Get it?'

To their astonishment their big catch just slapped leather-clad thighs with gloved hands and lowered himself to a boulder. He grinned philosophically and shook his head.

'Man, what a hooraw! You know, I thought twice about giving this scam a go, knowing a man could get himself killed in this neck of the woods. But then I convinced myself I could pull it off with just a lick of luck. Guess I never figured getting my big plan knocked on the head this way even before I got to try my big bluff.'

They stared in confusion. The Mexican accent was totally gone to be replaced by a straight mid-West drawl. Their prisoner appeared less scared than angry. Relieved almost. Most of all, he seemed no more dangerous now than one of the girls at the Green Rooms in town.

'Huh?' queried Hogan and McCall growled. 'What?'

They had no notion what was going on. What they did know was that the Rio Kid wasn't acting like any hired gun they'd ever come up against. But what was most disturbing was that their captive had used that word 'scam'. It was a term all too familiar to two men who of late had found themselves reduced to working small-beer scams themselves in order to stay solvent while waiting for their 'big chance' to happen along.

In this instance, Boss Caldwell had offered a $500 reward to anyone who could stop the high-priced Mex killer whom rival Roark Doolin was allegedly importing to gun him down, and Hogan and McCall had grabbed for it with eager assurance.

So far so good . . . maybe. But why

13

did they feel so distinctly uneasy as they studied their smiling, shrugging 'Mexican' perched on a rock before them?

Rio Kid didn't act like any kind of gunslinger, and plainly wasn't even remotely Mexican. And just what had he meant by 'scam' anyway?

Hogan cocked his .45.

McCall rammed his gunsights into the man's neck.

'Don't give us any crap,' warned Hogan.

'We're takin' you in pronto,' supported McCall. 'On your feet.'

'Well, you can do that if you really feel you gotta.' The Kid sighed, rising. He looked almost sympathetically from one to the other. 'But I sure doubt you'll get to collect. I mean, like I said, I never expected getting jumped like this. In my own interests I'd have to tell that cattleman my name is Arthur Higgins, otherwise he might do me in.'

Hogan wanted to start batting him about the head until he started talking straight, but McCall restrained him.

14

'Let's get this straight,' McCall grated. 'You're sayin' you're a fake?'

'Absolutely.'

'Bullshit!' Hogan's tone was venomous. They'd put a lot of time and effort into this caper, needed $500 the worst possible way. 'Caldwell is expectin' a flash-ass greaser *pistolero* and you're it. C'mon, let's get back to town and collect, Cade.'

'Won't do you any good I'm afraid, fellers,' insisted their man, spreading his hands. 'Look, I'll level with you and then mebbe you'll understand. You see, I heard about Caldwell sendin' for the Kid. But I knew the Kid was in the lock-up. So I saw a chance of masquerading as him and coming up and hitting the cattleman for a big advance, then getting gone before anybody was any the wiser. The big scam, you see. But now the game is up I'll tell the world I'm Arthur Higgins, and I can prove it.'

It sounded ominously like the truth. But suddenly Hogan attacked the man's saddle-bags, hurling neatly packed contents every which way as he searched for confirmation, one way or the other.

The pair found letters addressed to Arthur Higgins of Gravy City, Kansas. A collection of photographs depicting Arthur Higgins from childhood to the present. Similar various receipts, bills of sale and identification documents quickly put the matter of their prisoner's identity beyond all possible doubt. With the result that a short time later would-be con artist Arthur Higgins was on his way with one ear ringing from the bad tempered slap Hogan had just had to hand him before booting him into his saddle and pointing him back south the way he had come.

It was silent on that sundown ridge for a long and bitter time. The partners had played a long shot which evaporated in their hands in an unexpected and demoralizing way. Down on their uppers, no prospects and twenty miles from the nearest saloon, it felt as though they had reached a personal low as they watched the dot that was Higgins vanish in the evening haze, when something rustled in back of them.

It was a newspaper Higgins had failed to retrieve before his hasty exit. McCall collected it, studied it glumly. It was turned to a page 5 résumé of the range war which was outlined in pencil, doubtless by the Rio Kid's would-be impersonator.

With a sigh, McCall turned to Page I and his eyes popped.

'Well damn me to hell!' he breathed. 'They got Strabo!'

'What?'

Hogan snatched the paper from his hands. Sure enough, the report on the recent death at the hands of the law in Wolflock, Modoc County, carried 48-point headlines in the *Modoc Times* which read:

TRAIN BANDIT DIES BROKE!
STRABO SHOT DEAD IN SHERIFF'S
AMBUSH!

By this time, Hogan was clutching one page of the double spread and McCall the other. Together they scanned the account of 'great train robber' Cole Strabo's violent last shoot-out with riveted concentration, their silence absolute.

The late desperado had been neither relative nor pard. Yet Hogan and McCall had known the man briefly and dangerously long before he'd suddenly exploded into the glare of the big time the night he wrecked then robbed the High West Rail's Midnight Express a month earlier.

After some moments they lowered the newspaper to stare at one another in total silence.

This surely was the bottom of the bucket, the grinding of bitter sea-salt into wounded self-esteem and lost aspirations.

During their brief association with Cole Strabo the two had taken a violent dislike to his overbearing ways before the man eventually saw them off with the vitriolic parting shot that they were 'natural born tenth-raters who'd never amount to a hill of beans either straight or on the owlhoot'. It seemed that the outlaw's scathing assessment had possibly been borne out by Strabo's ascent to national prominence with the drama of the High West job, contrasting with their own corresponding descent into odd jobbing, horse-breaking, gambling and gunfighting — while all the time watching out for the big break.

Today they had failed again in a job which Strabo would have surely spurned as penny ante — the same day they had learned of that desperado's success against the railroad, even if it had eventually brought him to grief, as now revealed.

They felt so bad they couldn't even feel good that Strabo was now feeding the worms.

The long night ride across the lonesome plains was mostly silent apart from the occasional wistful speculation on the ultimate fate of Strabo's apparently still missing map of the Lost

Dutchman, the killer's prize for his attack on the express.

This comprehensive report in the *Modoc Times* reprised what two grudgingly avid followers of the late hellion's career already knew. Namely that sometime following the train robbery and the massive manhunt it generated, Strabo was rumoured to have dumped his regular bunch and apparently got off with the treasure map all to himself.

Typical Strabo, they'd thought at the time.

But now he was dead without any mention of the famous map. The two men who had shared just one brief and dangerous but memorable adventure with the late bandit king, before moderating some of their more reckless ways, could only stare up at the remote stars and ask the huge question:

Where was it now?

Eventually they agreed that crafty Strabo would never have lost the map, that tight-fisted Strabo would never have given it away or traded it, not at any price.

Which left just one sure certainty. He'd stashed it someplace.

And being the thoroughgoing pro he had always been, he'd doubtless done a highly efficient job of it, they agreed. You could bank on that.

'It's out there someplace, McCall,' Hogan stated. 'Someplace between Boston, Maine and good old LA. Simple when you say it quick.'

'Nobody will ever find it now,' insisted an even more bitter and demoralized Cade McCall. 'That map's gone with the big haul and Strabo — into eternity.'

That was a fitting mournful note on which to wind up on what had proved a long and bitterly disappointing day. By the time they turned in at the shabby back-street hotel of one-horse Clawhammer, which they could scarcely afford, all they wanted was the oblivion of sleep.

Cade McCall quickly found it. As a

consequence, he was sleep-befuddled and disgruntled when, some time later — he knew he couldn't have been asleep all that long — Hogan, obviously deranged by disappointment and failure, shook him violently awake and shouted meaninglessly in his face:

'Boot-heels, goddamnit! Boot-heels!'

McCall fumbled for his Colt but was too angry or befuddled to find it.

2

Pilgrim Law

No fire. Steak burnt dry in the skillet. Nobody to welcome a man home after a long morning's work at the jailhouse. No coffee. No chow. Nothing.

The sheriff of Wolflock fetched a fistful of kindling wood from the box by the stove and set about getting a fire going.

He knew what was going on, of course. This was all part of his punishment. Like himself, Clara Craddock had anticipated that the brilliant work he had done in identifying Cole Strabo's horse in a back lane that night, leading to the outlaw's apprehending and death, would inevitably result in his swift promotion and reassignment to someplace respectable and social such as North Platte, Grand Island or even

Lincoln itself for Sheriff Wal Craddock and spouse.

Instead, what did he have? A bullet-riddled corpse and not one sign of the by now famous Lost Dutchman map on the body or amongst Strabo's possessions. So he'd been commended, encouraged, made promises yet again — yet remained in Wolflock — maybe for ever.

Now, as though to add salt to his wounds, he'd been instructed to delay the burial of the outlaw in order that enough dignitaries might be mustered to attend the service and thereby reap the full publicity benefits of the occasion — which they kept insisting was no real occasion at all because of the failure to recover the map. What hypocrisy!

Where was the justice?

He kept blowing on his preparation of kindling, paper and wood before realizing the wood was damp.

Sheriff Craddock gave up and went through to the front room to drape his beanpole frame in his favorite big old chair by the wide-open windows, where he sat relaxed with his pipe with a lazy breeze blowing through the front room of his house.

Most days the Wolflock peace officer was to be found in this chair in his home around that time of the morning. He was by habit an early starter and late finisher on the streets, and lunch-hour was the time he gave himself to unwind and to pay a little attention to matters outside his work, such as his long-suffering wife.

Mrs Craddock was a climber who'd seen in tall Wal Craddock the makings of a big-city high sheriff or even marshal after he'd tamed raw and half-wild Wolflock on the fringe of the Dark Lands, deserts and the hostile Thousand Canyons country which lay beyond this last outpost of civilization, where men still died violently and the turpentine plant blew its fumes across the rooftops all day long.

If only . . . he mused. If only his

deputy had not missed Strabo's hard head with that bottle outside Anna Fran's side door, he could have arrested him, forced the secret of the map out of the man — the world would have been his oyster.

He was almost relieved when the somber rig hitched to a jet-black horse rolled to a stop at his garden gate and the cadaverous figure in black broadcloth got down stiffly to make his way down his pathway.

'That you, Sheriff?'

'Who else would it be?'

The visitor mounted the porch and peered at him through the window.

'He's got to be planted, Sheriff Craddock. I can't keep him much longer. Not in this weather, I can't.'

The sheriff deliberately gusted a big lungful of blue smoke out at Eternity Jones, who coughed and held a kerchief to his nose.

'No burial,' he stated. 'Not yet.'

'But, Sheriff, it's days now and we still haven't sighted any of those big-wigs from the capital. So why the delay?'

Disapproval clouded Wal Craddock's long and somber face. He was the rawboned descendant of a shambling race of hill men and tillers of the soil whose father had been a Boston policeman. The son had followed in the family tradition with distinction before resigning from the force to make his reputation on the wild frontier. Citizens such as the undertaker had total confidence in their peace officer, feared the day he might be promoted and moved on.

'That's for me to know and you to find out, Mr Jones.'

'But, Sheriff — '

'Ice, mister.'

'Huh?'

'Correct me if I'm wrong, undertaker, but don't you and Mr Carey of the drugstore keep a year-round ice supply down the old Arcadia mine for day-to-day needs in his case and emergencies in your own?'

'Oh yes, yes of course, Sheriff. Are you saying you want Mr Strabo — ?'

'Chilled.'

'But — '

'Preserved.'

'It will be costly, Sh — '

'Good day, Mr Jones.'

The undertaker was dismissed. He shuffled off down the path and Craddock had time to refill his pipe and think a few unkind thoughts about undertakers, wives and tricky badmen until the deputy showed at the fence.

'Well?' he murmured as the man reached the porch shade.

'Nothin', Sheriff.'

'You checked the hotels, roomers, back-street dives and the hobo jungles out along the tracks as I ordered?'

'The three of us have been doin' nothin' else all mornin'. Sure, there's new faces in town like always. But none that tallies with what we've got on Strabo's old bunch, sir.'

For the first time that day Wal Craddock allowed himself the luxury of a moment's dejection. He immediately thrust it aside, reminding himself of the plan he'd come up with which just might — might lead him to a link with the Map — namely prospector Barney Brown's by now famous location map of the Lost Dutchman mine for which men had searched for years somewhere out in the nightmare heart of the Thousand Canyons region to the west.

He was banking his hopes now on what the press liked to identify as an Outlaw's Funeral.

Such ceremonials were a Western tradition. When a badman of status cashed in, it was the custom for friends and foes alike of the Dark Brotherhood to forget past differences with the deceased, drop what they were doing, put on their Sunday best and roll up to ensure that one of their number was farewelled in fitting style.

Sheriff Craddock was staking everything on the slender hope that somebody connected with Strabo might find themselves unable to resist the temptation of farewelling the killer in the traditional way, might show up for the big funeral and fall into his hands.

He didn't give a rap if the officials from the county seat made it here for the interment or not. He was hungry to snare just one of the dead man's henchmen; it only took one to sing.

Yet with days drifting by and not so much of a whiff of a Hodge, Sanger, Doone or the fearsome Erskine yet to be sighted, he was feeling disappointed.

He refused to let it show.

'Carry on, Deputy,' he said briskly. 'And make sure you meet the 2.30 from the north this afternoon. I want every new arrival checked and double-checked.'

'Yes, sir!'

Soon the sheriff was back on the streets, taking the long way back to Front via the south trail and the turpentine plant.

Wolflock had been a wild sawmill town in the early post-war years, but the cut-over land, the towering heaps of gray sawdust and the rusting and rotting mill-flumes told how it had begun to die.

Five years ago the place had been virtually comatose. Then came the railroad, the vital link with the outside world and the essential artery for the town's prime industry, the turpentine plant.

The plant stood on the southern limits of the town, its stacks billowing smoke and grime across a town slowly but surely beginning to prosper a second time by virtue of new people and new enterprises. There were several new hotels and saloons, and while a number of people still made a living grubbing the pine-stumps from the ground, most were engaged in such fields as transport, ranching and ancillary occupations.

What had not changed significantly over the years was the nature of the place and the character of its people. Isolated, close to the wild desert regions and with a violent history, this was a broad-shouldered town with a chip on its shoulder, a resentment for authority and ready to erupt at the slightest hint of trouble.

Many believed that only Craddock stood between this town and chaos; one man who believed that was Craddock himself.

The irony at present was that his destruction of a notorious outlaw had made Wolflock an even more dangerous place to be. The whiff of a $50,000 fortune in mined gold had brought them along in droves — fortune-hunters, scavengers, desert rats, drifters, saddle bums and hard men with faces straight off wanted dodgers. All fired by the desperate hope that somewhere, somehow the treasure map that men had murdered to obtain, might show.

He shrugged at the thought, focused on a strongly held belief.

Someone apart from Strabo himself had to know where that priceless strip of deerskin was to be found. He refused to believe otherwise. That man would eventually show, and Craddock would see to the rest. But you couldn't have an Outlaw's Funeral without the outlaw. Therefore, Strabo's corpse simply had remained on show to attract the hellions to town. So Eternity Jones had better quit worrying about what ice was costing him these days.

★ ★ ★

The horses travelled easily along the old Mulberry Trail where it climbed out of the valley and swung through the foothills north of Parlee.

'Yonder's Blue Mountain,' McCall called above the clatter of hoofs. 'Can't see Cloverville from here but we know it's there.'

'Ain't likely to forget Cloverville,' Hogan agreed, fingering the brown flat brim back off his broad forehead. 'Especially not now, huh?'

McCall nodded. But for Cloverville they wouldn't be out on this high trail now, heading west for Modoc County and Wolflock.

It had been a day much like this several years back which had seen two young hell-raisers and one genuine denizen of the owlhoot come together by chance between towns, between troubles and between a fording across the River Dee and a nowhere hick town named Cloverville . . .

That day had been hot and Cole Strabo was dozing on a river bank when he heard the sound of horses on the trail, making for the fording nearby.

In one rippling move the outlaw was out of sight with a sixgun in his fist and narrowed eyes focused on the trail as five men sporting badges rode into sight.

Strabo cursed as he backed deeper into the brush and eased downslope towards the water.

They'd been hounding him all week, these lawmen from Murdock. It had to do with yet another failed express office stick-up which had netted him nothing but the attention of a long-nosed Murdock marshal and four deputies.

34

As silent and stealthy as a timber wolf, the tall outlaw crouched behind a big wateroak with his gun still in his fist, listening to the sound of receding hoofbeats, when he jumped a foot at a close voice.

'You too, eh, buddy?'

The outlaw whirled to confront a grinning Cade McCall and a sober Link Hogan. The pair were grimed from head to toe as a result of long days on the run following an incident up-river in which shots had been exchanged, punches thrown and a peace officer dumped on his backside. This had resulted in a headlong pursuit which to the pursued seemed out of all proportion to what they regarded as nothing much worse than a good night's fun that had gotten slightly out of hand.

Strabo knew nothing of this. All he knew was that this pair of strangers had been skilled enough and nervy enough to get within spitting distance of him without his having heard a damn thing.

The badman was impressed, which was why he didn't shoot first and ask questions later. Instead he had them identify themselves, then boastingly admitted his identity, adding proudly that he was wanted in at least six states and territories.

Eventually the lawmen drifted off and fell silent. Strabo leaned against a tree-trunk and studied his new acquaintances critically. They almost looked like outlaws, he mused. But looks could be deceptive. For in reality the two were just fiddle-footed youngsters with ambitions and big ideas who, despite their current problems with the law, looked and sounded more like regular Westerners than genuine hardcases, such as Strabo.

He assessed them as likely-looking, probably tough enough yet still almost certainly small-time and incompetent. That was sufficient reason to ditch his new 'friends', which he was about to do when they heard the sound of riders higher up along the river bluffs.

'Who the hell — ?' he hissed, squinting upslope through the foliage.

'Possemen!' keen-eyed McCall said in a perfunctory way. 'If they ain't the dogs runnin' us, they're the ones after you, Cole. You want to sweat it here or hightail?'

It was at that point that Strabo's diminishing respect for the younger men dropped several more notches. For the Dee curved sharply here, and the possemen were on the bluffs in command of the curve. With the full-running river at their backs the three had noplace to hightail to.

He said as much, but Link Hogan made a dismissive gesture.

'We got a boat, Strabo,' he said cockily, jerking a thumb over his shoulder. 'Wanna try it?'

It took Strabo no longer than just seconds to reach a decision. That was sufficient time to conjure up images of arrest, trial and a slow climb up thirteen steps to a gallows platform to repay a debt to Justice on counts ranging from running a rigged roulette wheel to murder.

The boat it would be.

It was sheer rotten luck that stopped him recording yet another daring escape from the foul and grasping claws of the law.

The three skimmed through the fording unseen and were gliding around the next bend, seemingly home free, when they sighted the marshal's horse. The horse had bogged in the river shallows, otherwise the whole party would have been up on the bluffs with the possemen tracking Hogan and McCall.

There were five lawmen in the bunch attempting to extricate the stressed animal. Startled momentarily by the sudden appearance of three equally alarmed badmen in a silly little boat, the badgemen recovered smartly enough to throw down on the trio, who were sitting ducks out in there in the middle of the river, in a boat threatening to capsize at any moment.

An hour later saw three hog-tied 'desperadoes' hunkered down on the hard floorboards of the enclosed cage of the prison van carrying them for Cloverville. One lawman drove while two deputies rode up top cradling shotguns in their laps.

Hogan and McCall were blaming Lady Luck for their misfortune, but Strabo blamed them.

They were idiots, millstones, bad-luckers and born-to-hang greenhorns, he accused. They had succeeded in doing in half an hour what the combined law agencies of six territories had failed to do over five years, he accused, namely, bagging Cole Strabo.

Deep in a blue mood, McCall was willing to let the badman sound off all he wanted if it made him feel any better, even if he reckoned the outlaw was acting about as ungrateful as a man could be. Hogan was less forgiving.

'You reckon it's been brains and knowhow that's kept you out of the law's clutches all this time, mister? You got to be jokin'!'

'And just what do you mean by that?' came the snarling reply. Intimidated, McCall wished Hogan would drop it, but knew that was asking too much.

'Meanin',' Hogan said deliberately, leaning toward the desperado, 'the John Laws hereabouts say they could nab you any old time they wanted, only a man with your record for fouled-up jobs just ain't worth it, especially when they got real outlaws to catch.'

Strabo's eyes flared hot. Although bound hand and foot, he had enough power and bad temper to hurl his big body into Hogan in a tigerish lunge. Poled over onto his back by the impact, Hogan somehow managed to double up his legs then snapped his boots into the man's chest. The impact hurled Strabo backwards to smash into the gunnel rail with sickening force. His eyes rolled in their sockets and he sagged forwards and hit the floorboards with his face like he was out to the world.

'Enough, goddamnit!' bawled McCall as the driver sawed back on the reins. 'You want to kill him and have the judge tack murder on to us as well?'

Hogan ignored him. His blood was up. He attempted to kick the motionless figure in the head where he lay slumped on the floor. He missed. He was too angry to be accurate. Next moment he was gasping and choking as a powerful arm whipped around his throat from behind and slammed the back of his head into a stanchion, filling his head with shooting stars.

Strabo had been playing possum.

He jerked upright and head-butted the captive Hogan in the face. McCall kicked him in the crotch. By the time the badgemen had stopped the van, Strabo still had a stranglehold on Hogan while McCall was trying to break his grip by kicking him in the small of his back.

Black billy-clubs rose and fell rhythmically. Hard heads bowed beneath the brutal fusillade. By the time the

41

deputies got through and the van was under way once more, the three were battered, bleeding and sore as boils, yet two at least were unrepentant.

'Tenth-rater!'

'Show pony.'

'Snot-nosed punk!'

'Has-been!'

Leaning his back against a wall of the security cage, where they didn't require to be bound, McCall serviced a bloody nose with his kerchief in disgust. He was prepared to just let them wrangle this time, should they start up again. To hell with them!

Hot-headed Hogan was willing to go on with it, but Strabo abruptly withdrew to a corner where he sat taking scowling, deep breaths, composing himself. Hogan hurled another insult which went unchallenged. Only when the outlaw eventually began fiddling with his boots did he break his silence, voice calm, his meaning mysterious:

'Thank your lucky stars I've only got

two shots, punk.'

'Huh?' muttered Hogan. He looked quizzically at McCall, who appeared puzzled in response: What was the badman talking about? Two shots? Maybe the billy-clubs had done more damage to Strabo's head than was apparent.

Then they realized that, as though by sleight of hand, the outlaw had unscrewed both high heels from his fancy boots. They were silent as he dug into what were revealed as hollow heels to produce firstly the butt-and-trigger assembly of some kind of small weapon from one, matched up by a gleaming chamber and stubby barrel from the other.

Their jaws sagged as the outlaw clicked the sections together before proudly holding up a fat and deadly little two-shot .22, cocked and ready to fire. His eyes gleamed with malice yet his big-toothed smile in the gloom seemed to temper his venom. In truth, he now seemed to be displaying something almost approaching brutal good humor.

And why not?

'Like I say, hardnose,' he drawled at Hogan, 'only got two bullets. And you just ain't worth one. So why don't you earn your keep and start bangin' on that door, boy? And you, McCall, you get ready to pitch in just in case it comes to shootin' and I need a husky feller around your size to chime in and back my play. Well, what are you settin' there lookin' like horse-apples for? You want to make a break before we hit town, or after?'

Hogan and McCall traded stunned looks. Next instant, Hogan was hammering on the door and shouting at the top of his lungs that Strabo was trying to kill them. Again. For the second time the lumbering van groaned to a halt, and deputies' curses and threats filled the air as the padlock was again unbolted and slid back, enabling the cage hatch to be jerked open.

As it fell back a long arm clutching a

pistol shot through the opening and the muzzle of the sneak gun was rammed hard into the first deputy's fat mouth.

As luck would have it, the deputy was yellow right through. The moment he recognised his peril, he froze in fear, so alarming his companions that an eager Hogan and McCall were able to surge out and overpower them beneath the cover of Strabo's gun, with scarcely a punch thrown or a groin-kick landed.

They were gone within moments, Strabo to build his murderous reputation on the owlhoot, the partners to make their peace with the John Laws and stop brawling in public places — at least for a while.

That exhilarating day of peril and excitement was still a keen memory one dark night several months later, and had been the direct cause of Hogan jolting up from a half-sleep groaning 'Boot-heels! Boot-heels!'

By the time he'd explained the significance of his dream and deftly connected it with their current preoccupation with a map which might prove either totally mythical or all too real, dawn was breaking over a rugged landscape. As a result, the sunny day that followed found them riding fast for Wolflock but thinking about another town named Cloverville.

An excited Hogan had by this time totally convinced himself that: one, there had to be a map, and: two, that they were going to locate it in those hollow heels of Cole Strabo's boots. His vivid dream-recollection of the Cloverville incident now reassured him that they needed only to do what must be done quietly, calmly and hyper-efficiently for the precious *derrotero* to fall into their laps.

'It's in the bag, partner,' he insisted with a wide grin. 'We're the chosen ones. We were destined to get tangled up with Strabo that day simply and solely to find out about his goddamn boot-heels. It's fate and kismet and the goddamn Easter rabbit.' He paused with a frown. 'Say, what are you like at diggin'?'

Hogan knew what he meant. By this time, Strabo should be well and truly six feet under.

But he wasn't.

3

Tough Enough

There was a languid laziness about that morning with the sun well above the rooftops and a quality in the air that did not hold the dust as the trio rounded the corner from Pearl Street and strolled along Main.

Men lounged in groups along the boardwalk in the central block, leaning against the hitch rails and propping up the storefronts, watching the women go by but not taking too much notice until they sighted Anna Fran with her escorts. Conversations faded and heads turned as the trio moved into a slant of sunlight falling along the street across from the Wolflock Feed and Grain, for the Green Rooms' star attraction was by far the most admired woman in town. Strangely, Hogan and McCall enjoyed an almost equal popularity, although for markedly different reasons. Although relatively law-abiding these days, the pair had about them an air of reckless daring and bravado which, supported by good looks and reputations, cast them as unlikely role models for the younger generation, and objects of envy for older men soaking up the sun.

As usual the sight of the three coming in from Anna Fran's street at this time of the morning revived the gossip. Were they a threesome? Had Link and Cade stayed at her place overnight? Such was the interest the walkers aroused amongst the strollers, porch-loafers and storekeepers soaking up the sun on their stoops before the day's business got properly under way.

But, unaware of the attention, the trio were deep in conversation, and several porch-loafers distinctly heard Link Hogan say: 'If they'd found it everybody'd know about it. You couldn't keep something that big quiet . . . '

Ears pricked. Were they discussing

the topic dominating every store, saloon and street these uncertain days, namely 'the Map'?

The legend of the Dutchman pervaded the atmosphere of rough-and-ready Wolflock like a mist that never blew away. It was part of its culture and at present the town was a hotbed of gossip and speculation related to Strabo's death and whether or not they'd found the missing *derrotero* on him when he died.

The eavesdroppers would have been disappointed to know that Hogan's remark had actually only been in reference to a rumor going about that the owners of the Plains Hotel were reputedly considering putting the place up for sale, a rumor that Anna Fran found particularly exciting, considering they shared a probably foolish preoccupation with that place.

'How much, Link?' she asked eagerly as they passed the post office where a poster of Strabo still glowered down.

'I didn't hear, Anna. Bulk *dinero*, I'd

hazard, though. What do you calculate, man?'

'Ten thousand, mebbe?' speculated McCall, gazing ahead at the impressive bulk of the hotel. He cocked an eyebrow at the girl. 'You sure Strabo didn't even drop one itt-bitty hint about where he might have stashed that gol-durned *derrotero*, little woman?'

'I've already told you!' Anna Fran almost snapped. 'He said nothing. Don't you trust me?'

'We'd sure like to, honey,' said Hogan, feeling like a hypocrite. For he and McCall were nursing a plan for tracking down that map which they hadn't confided to her.

He caught his partner's eye but McCall just looked blank. So he switched the conversation to something else and they continued on their way, enjoying the golden morning, all three vain enough to be now fully aware of the attention they attracted as they strolled on by the blacksmith's on the opposite side of the street. They completely spoiled the sheriff's morning.

'Oh yeah?' growled the blacksmith.

'Yeah!' affirmed the sheriff. 'You heard me loud and clear, mister. Shift that horse off the walk.'

'Says who?'

'Says the law, mister.'

'What if I don't?'

That was outright defiance if ever Craddock had heard it. He wouldn't stand for that, or at least not in his present mood he wouldn't.

The lawman's flinty gaze flickered momentarily after the receding trio on the far side of the street, and he felt a taste like acid against his teeth.

Some folks claimed Wal Craddock, the married man and pillar of church and law had designs on Anna Fran Hellinger. That wasn't true. Craddock would stay wed to ambitious Mrs Craddock until the end — unless she up and left him. But that didn't stop him admiring a young woman of class and spirit, or resenting it whenever he saw her with that pair, who were so damned young, handsome — and shady, in his book.

It was bad enough that the girl seemed attached, not just to one, but both. And he'd heard the whispers that the three of them were ... hell! He wasn't going to think about that.

He returned his attention to a problem he could deal with.

'It's against city ordinances to allow any animal to obstruct any public thoroughfare, blacksmith.' He jabbed the hindquarters of the offending percheron with his forefinger. 'Shift it and shift it now!'

'There you go again, Craddock. You still think you're back in Boston with tramcars runnin' down the streets and everyone decked out in satins and silks. This is the West, you stiff-necked son of a bitch. You might be an okay lawman, but when are you goin' to learn that you can't — '

'Can and will, mister!' Craddock

barked, and slammed the smith's hairy chest with the heels of his hands, sending him teetering backwards to land into his oil-streaked cooling-tub with a mighty splash.

Afterwards, onlookers would comment that, although they were accustomed to Wal Craddock's rigid ways and testy temper, it seemed their peace officer was getting ornerier by the day of late. Why was this so?

Now Craddock kicked the sole of one of the sodden smith's big number twelves as he tried to lever himself out of the greasy water.

'Next time a fifty-dollar fine and if there's a time after that — the slammer. You got that?'

'Er, yessir, Sheriff Craddock, sir. Have a good day, sir.'

Craddock looked his familiar grim-jawed self as he turned away. Confrontation and action could have that effect on him.

Yet that crack about Boston rankled, for many here and in the county capital believed he'd never made the adjustment from the East Coast to Nebraska. His enemies and detractors claimed he actually hated the West and wouldn't rest until he'd moulded it to his satisfaction. Maybe they were right when citizens claimed he only saw wildness, outlawry and sin where they saw improvement, optimism and a West they could be proud of.

He stepped through the jailhouse doorway and immediately grabbed for his sixgun.

'It's all right, Sheriff!' yelled his second deputy. 'We rounded 'em up.'

Four hard-bitten strangers stood lined up before the sheriff's desk. Craddock's nose crinkled. He smelt owlhoot immediately. Broken noses, gaudy suits and sagging holsters, with cigar-smoke polluting the office air, made it look like a hardcase convention.

'What the hell — ?' he muttered. Then he stopped, remembering his orders to the effect that all suspicious persons arriving in town prior to the impending Strabo funeral were to be brought in for identification and examination.

'What the hell is this?' demanded the broken-nose with the black cigar. 'What are we supposed to have done, damnit?'

Craddock snatched the cigar from hairy fingers and flipped it through the door into the street where it sank in the dust as though in water.

Broken-nose backed up. All did. They'd been forewarned about the sheriff of Wolflock.

Having asserted his authority, Craddock immediately set about an exhaustive interrogation: names, aliases, addresses, purpose of visit, connection if any with the deceased Cole Strabo.

Half an hour later, he threw them out. There was no doubt in his mind that all were outlaws of one stripe or another. All admitted having known the deceased — which was the reason they were here. As far as the jailhouse records revealed, none of the group was wanted in Modoc County by the law at that particular time, although Craddock's instincts told him they had to be wanted someplace.

But by the time he was through with the bunch, Craddock was convinced that none corresponded to the names and descriptions of four long riders named Erskine, Hodge, Sanger or Doone, now known to have been Strabo's associates in the attack upon the Midnight Express. That crime preoccupied him these days.

'Coffee!' he barked, and it quickly appeared. Then: 'Report!' and two of his three deputies proceeded to bring him up to date on the latest from streets and office.

Hesitant steps on the porch. A shadow fell through the sunlit doorway and the biggest and toughest of the four detainees stood there, glowering.

'Forgot me hat.'

'We're not here to pick up for the likes of you,' Craddock growled. 'Get it yourself.'

Badman Dave Tutt was wanted in many places but not here in Nebraska. As he collected his piece and turned to go, the sheriff came out of his chair and blocked his path. They stood chest to chest, just as Craddock had done with the blacksmith.

'What's the scuttlebutt, Tutt?'

'Huh?'

'I know you can't talk freely in front of your moron friends. But now I want to know what they're saying on the owlhoot trails these days. Where do snakes like you really reckon that *derrotero* is?'

Tutt sneered.

Craddock's right fist slammed into a hard chin. 'Tough Dave', they called Tutt elsewhere, yet all veneer of toughness vanished as he sagged to his knees.

'None of us knows nothin', I swear, Sheriff,' he slurred thickly. 'If we did we'd be out there lookin' for it. But I'll admit I come here for the funeral hopin' I might hear a whisper on what

Strabo done with that map. But nobody knows a blue-eyed thing, not here, not anyplace. You can't kill a man for bein' ignorant, Sheriff.'

'You're right,' Craddock said woodenly, contemptuously. 'Get up and get out.'

Craddock examined a skinned knuckle. Was he losing his grip? Was he banking too heavily on solving the mystery of the lost *derrotero*?

A wary head peeped around the doorframe. The junior deputy. The sheriff was beginning to scare his own people.

'Sheriff.'

'Huh?'

Craddock's manner was vague. He was reflecting on the encouraging fact that at last big-time outlaws were starting to show up for the funeral; just as he had hoped. Now that the Tutt bunch was here he had every right to expect more would show, providing he delayed the funeral long enough. After some moments he stared at the deputy.

'Yes, what is it?'

'You've got another visitor, Sheriff.'

'Not this morning, I haven't. I mean to go back over every single word we've got on Strabo and his bunch until . . . '

He stopped talking. Anna Fran Hellinger could have that effect on a man, even the sheriff. Then he reminded himself that it had been his .45 which had blasted life from the body of a badman, still warm from this girl's arms.

'Ahh, yes?' he asked stiffly. She came straight to the point.

'I've come to ask the reason behind the delay with the burying, Sheriff.'

'Why not? No big hurry, is there?'

'It's not fitting.'

He leaned forward sharply, eyebrows hooking upwards like twin question marks.

'Is there some good reason you want to see that hellion put in the ground, girl? That makes me wonder if mebbe you know something you aren't telling. Maybe you are just waiting for the funeral so that you can run off with that damned map without attracting suspicion. Is that how it is?'

'Why'd you have to kill him?' she flared.

'The low-down son of a bitch would have surely killed us if we hadn't.'

'You're so hard, Sheriff Craddock.'

'And you, Miss Hellinger, are a consort of badmen and a disgrace to a decent town.'

She rose unruffled and, with a saucy smile for the eavesdropping deputies, left them scratching their heads.

You never knew about Anna Fran, the lawmen reflected. She was bewitchingly unpredictable and unreadable, always seemed to be one jump ahead. And they wondered, watching her figure recede along Front, whether Strabo might, in a moment of intimacy perhaps, have whispered something in her shell-pink ear about that *derrotero* that had the whole Territory speculating.

Unfortunately for Anna Fran, he hadn't.

The girl remained deeply disappointed about this. Strabo had meant less than nothing to her, yet she chose to play the grieving intimate role to afford herself legitimate cover for staying close to the main game in town, namely the search for a lead on the Lost Dutchman.

Today she'd hoped to jolt something out of Craddock which he might be keeping from the general public, but she had left more convinced than ever that he knew no more than herself. On his last night, Strabo had swaggered from her house directly into a Colt massacre without dropping one word on the *derrotero*.

The whole ugly affair was almost enough to make a woman give up on her big dreams of being rich some day. Almost, but not quite.

Anna Fran had quit her home back East and set out to conquer the West any way she could.

That ambition still burned now as she approached the building with the hand-lettered sign which read: Heavenly Rest Funeral Parlor.

She found the undertaker slumped behind his big black mahogany desk in the carpeted reception lobby. He sprang erect with a lecherous smile.

'Anna Fran! What a pleasant surprise. Do take a seat, my dear.' He smiled broadly before remembering that he harboured the remains of the man who had spent his final hours with this vision from the high side of town. He almost envied Strabo even if he was dead. He yearned for her soft white body himself. 'How may I help you?'

'You can tell me why the delay in announcing the funeral date, Joachim?'

'Sheriff's orders, I'm afraid, my dear. He has his reasons, I suppose.'

'How long can you keep the . . . umm . . . remains?'

'A question occupying me at this very moment, m'dear. Not much longer — might be as close as I can say. There is also the matter of space. I expect you would like to see your friend laid to rest as soon as possible?'

Anna Fran leaned forward. 'He was a low outlaw, Joachim.'

'Oh? But I thought you — '

'An outlaw worth a fortune.' Anna Fran put on her best smile. 'Joachim, as an old friend, you would confide in me if you had seen or found anything on Strabo that might indicate what he did with his valuables, wouldn't you? You see, the night he died he promised to me a share of whatever he found in the Lost Dutchman. He said he loved me. I'm sure he meant it. So, was there anything?'

A windy sigh. 'The sheriff and I went through everything, even examined the body head to toe. Nothing. The sheriff was bitterly disappointed, as I'm sure you are to hear this. I suppose I would have been also had I any interest in that so-called El Dorado, which of course I haven't.'

Eternity Jones could lie like a snake-oil salesman. But he told the truth about the *derrotero*. He had gone over that bullet-riddled corpse with a magnifying glass, but there had been nothing remotely connected to the map. Not a dicky bird.

'Well,' she said, rising to go, 'if anything should turn up . . . '

'I shall pass it on to you immediately.'

He would not, of course. Should anything turn up, Eternity would be out the door and *en route* to wherever the remote compass point was, somewhere in the Thousand Canyons region, where a big-nosed little fossicker named Barney Brown had uncovered the Dutchman's golden secret. If he found it, it would be his. All his. Anna Fran might be a lonely undertaker's impossible vision of youth and beauty. But old Barney's mine was the stuff that dreams were made of . . .

Death, money and lust might well rule Eternity's life, but lust always ran a bad third.

After she had gone he went through to the workroom. He stopped, sniffing. The ice really wasn't working. And he was indeed getting crowded out. Sooner or later something would have to be done. He already had some ideas on how to deal with the current problem, which should satisfy all concerned, providing they didn't know what was really going on.

He crossed the room to speak Marcus the embalmer. Marcus was working on the Widow McAllister. The two men discussed the 'myth' of the Lost Dutchman. It was a topic greedy men never wearied of.

* * *

Night was falling. The skies to the west were beautifully serene. Small fleecy pink clouds delicately edged with gold were sailing like ships across the dark purple of the evening sky, the next moment taking on the shape of swans, then fantastic monsters. Between the tall trees could be seen the rising hills, the last of the light painting them colors you might only ever get to see in

Nebraska and at this time of year.

Link Hogan sighed and cast his mind ahead.

The Lost Dutchman might yet prove to be just another in a long list of scrapes, scams and big deals that had attracted him over the years. You took a chance, ran some risks, kept your focus on the main game and at the end you stood either to waltz off with a big piece of money or maybe wind up in jail or the grave.

He looked ahead. Smoke trailed back over McCall's shoulder. He was humming a tune they'd heard in Kearney last visit. His partner was happy. Always was when there was something big in the offing, even if this current possibility might prove their most improbable long shot ever.

'Hey, Cade.'

McCall looked over his shoulder. 'What?'

'Ever think about it these days?'

'About what?'

'You know. Goin' straight.'

McCall's good-looking, short-nosed American face lighted up with a big grin.

'You never let me down, do you, *amigo*.'

'Why. What do you mean?'

'Well, no matter how boring life might get, I can always count on you to come up with something loco to break the monotony.'

'You mean, something loco like going straight?'

'Hey, hey . . . you and me goin' straight, man. Doesn't get much crazier than that, does it?'

He was right, Hogan reflected behind a fading smile. It was crazy. The only thing he could dream of that might ever encourage him to quit riding on the shady side of the law might be a grubstake he could parlay into a business or trade that would set them free to kick off the old ways for keeps. He didn't really want the world.

He realized he could see the lights of Wolflock winking far ahead as darkness overtook them from the east.

4

Bad Moon Rising

A bunch of horsemen appeared out-lined against the crimson backwash of the plains where the sun had died a slow death twenty minutes earlier. They rode wearily but warily and didn't speak until they glimpsed the camp-fires of the Kansas — Colorado railroad crews flickering in the darkness a mile ahead.

'Grub.'

Doone, the youngest of the outlaw gang, was never totally free of hunger, thirst or both. Hunger for roast meat and cream pies, thirst for cold water and lemonade, rye whiskey and beer — all never-ending and free.

But he would settle for bread and goat cheese at a railroaders' camp if that was the best offering.

'Steak,' responded Sanger, his voice a nasal twang roughened by thirst and trail dust. 'Rich and juicy is how I want it, with peach ice-cream for dessert, by God!'

'You guys beat all,' growled barrel-chested Hodge, bigger than Doone and even meaner than hill man Hodge. 'We run forty miles of posse country and all you can think of is your bellies. Me? I'll chow down at Wolflock, not before. Eh, Phil?'

Phil Erskine, leader by default of what was once known as the Strabo Bunch, grunted, coughed and brought up trail dust. They were played out and run ragged. News of Strabo's death had caught up with them as they were following a false lead on the notorious map far to the south. Heading back north had led them into an exhausting running battle with a string of posses hunting for some rustling outfit which apparently loosely fitted their description.

It had taken days to sneak across the

border back into Nebraska, days in which they were nervously conscious of every tick of the clock, every small sound, every bend in the road. Strabo was dead and the ghouls would be picking over his bones in search of a lead on the *derrotero*. And a treasure they regarded as theirs by right, now maybe was lost for ever. Erskine was so bitter about the manner in which first Strabo and then circumstances had conspired against him, that all he was capable of doing right now was to growl like some wild animal and think solely about food.

He would fret about everything else later.

The railroaders proved to be rough, bearded, hospitable. They invited the travel-weary four to break bread with them and didn't ask questions. If they tagged them as owlhoot, nobody commented. They weren't peace officers or even peace-loving citizens down here along the bleak steel of the Kansas and Colorado line. Just hard men trying to make a buck. Like Erskine and his crew.

'Now I'm full I just want to sleep,' grunted Doone an hour later. He stretched out on an oilskin before the small fire they'd built some distance from the nearest camp. A buffalo-hump supper had left his face greasy and deeply creased with exhaustion. 'Who's got tobacco?'

That was how hard up they were. Half-starving and low on weed. They thought they'd had it rough when Strabo was leading them from one penny ante job to another. But this was the real thing. They had run themselves into the ground hunting for a Strabo who was unknowingly heading for his own apocalypse far away. Slogging north, they'd sensed their prospects of finding good fortune or anything resembling it in Modoc County dimming by the hour.

They now sprawled by a smoking fire on a black soil prairie looking for the booster that would get them up and riding one more time.

And half-asleep from exhaustion, some mused dreamily how vastly different it had been the last time they had hunkered down to chow together by a long curving sweep of the High Iron . . . and memory carried them all the way back to a night none would ever forget . . .

* * *

The rails were humming.

Strabo heard it first. Faintly, barely perceptible yet undeniable now, the shining steel tracks veering around the looming landmark of Red Horse Rock were faintly trembling under the onrushing weight of steel wheels carrying loco, tender and paycar swiftly towards them through the misting night.

Doone was a cynic and a doubter. He didn't actually believe it until he placed his hand on the rail and actually felt the Midnight Express sending him the rhythmic message through his finger-tips. Here I come. Here I come.

The broad-shouldered young heller leapt up and trotted off towards the timber-laden two-mule wagon tied up under the moonwashed liveoaks nearby.

Not for Doone any queasy concerns about sacrificing a couple of healthy mules upon the altar of greed. This was the big one. He would gladly see a hundred blood Arabian thoroughbreds chewed up and spat out under impla-cable steel wheels tonight if that was what it took to get a shot at a payday the size of the one Strabo was predicting tonight.

The key to the Lost Dutchman!

Were they really that tantalizingly close to what seemed even to them like something spun from myth?

And what a myth!

A solitary prospector drifts off into a nightmare land of trackless canyons and painted savages and uses twenty years of his life to uncover at last a seam of yellow gold. He mines it and eventually exhausts the seam. He covers his tracks and heads back to civilization to stake his claim and figure out just how he might get to ship his fortune out into the white man's world without losing his scalp, his hair, and his life.

He doesn't make it. The Choctaw get him on his return journey and the chief uses the curiously marked strip of soft leather found on the body as a headdress ornament. Years later the chief dies in battle with the Bluecoats and the piece of leather eventually falls into the hands of a man who realizes that it is what Mexican prospectors call a *derrotero*, namely a chart or a map.

In this case an intricately detailed map, showing the route to an isolated spot far out in the Thousand Canyons country identified only by an X.

Fortune-hunter and prospector Barney Brown reckoned it was worth following up. Several months later he found himself seated in a man-made cavern beneath the earth at the head of a played-out shaft and surrounded by sacks of yellow gold — mined, bagged and secreted by the Dutchman long ago.

Barney was tough, cagey and knew how to keep a secret. But a fortune in yellow gold can have a voice of its own that seems to whisper on the winds, and when the rumor of his find somehow escaped, grizzled Barney realized he must be prepared to share his secret with others and agree to settle for less than the total prize, otherwise he might well share the Dutchman's fate.

The deal was struck with the bank at Fort Cromwell. The bank would finance the transport of the gold to its vaults and share with Barney fifty-fifty.

The whole expensive process of recovering and transporting the Dutchman's gold from its hiding-place would be conducted by the bank some time after Barney had delivered, in person, the all-important *derrotero* to their headquarters.

Barney laid the plans for his trip with his precious map up to Fort Cromwell with infinite caution and maximum secrecy. But who could exclusively hire a loco, tender, armor-plated coach and a dozen top-flight security guards without someone's tongue slipping up somewhere along the line?

It simply wasn't possible. And any man with that sort of information at his fingertips realized quickly just how valuable it would be to men of a certain persuasion — such as bloody-handed outlaw gangs like Strabo's, for instance.

Now, at a place where the tracks climbed high and trains were forced to slow by the gradient, dark figures were running for horses and guns as the first whipping beam of headlight flickered through tall trees.

'Get them critters movin', Doone!' bawled Strabo as he leapt astride his big horse. No masks. It wasn't going to be that kind of a hold-up. Strabo's plan was that there would be no survivors. 'What the hell are you waitin' for?'

Doone was already laying leather onto the mules which didn't move them one inch closer to the tracks. The animals were both scared and stubborn. They could hear the train, didn't like the way moonlight glinted off the shivering rails and were even prepared to ignore the vicious cut of leather ribbons across dusty backs rather than budge.

'I told you this was a bad idea, Cole!' Slim Sanger was a hill man. Grew up with mules. Liked them. Understood them even. His hard-won philosophy was that a man could always count on a mule — count on it to let you down. Like this pair were doing right now. He couldn't figure why Strabo hadn't listened to him when they were laying their plans.

He was almost knocked from his saddle as Strabo grazed him as he stormed by on his big horse, bellowing to the others to follow him. All hands immediately laid into the mules with quirts and sticks as the train rounded the last bend and flooded the granite bulk of Red Horse Rock with light from its mirrored headlamp.

It remained a man-versus-mule stalemate until Strabo suddenly spurred back to the camp-fire. Leaning low from the saddle, Indian style, he snatched up a burning brand and came galloping back, urged on by his companions when they sensed his intent.

The mules rolled their eyes wildly. With a train thundering their way from one direction and a rider with a mean look in his eye closing in fast, brandishing something red-hot and smoking, the agitated critters were pitching and slewing every which way except straight ahead — until the racing rider reached them.

Strabo was as uncomplicated as a bullet. The instant he reached the first teamer he rammed the burning stick viciously into its rump, sending up an immediate plume of smoke.

The mule jumped ten feet and came down running, dragging the other with it. The sudden plunging motion almost jolted Doone off his seat but he managed to regain his balance and whipped the pair right up to the very tracks themselves before making a spectacular leap into mid-air.

Doone hit earth in the same instant that the Express crashed into the heavily weighted rig.

Only redneck Slim Sanger glanced away from the grisly spectacle as a forty-ton locomotive ploughed head-long into two mules and a one-ton wagon at thirty-five miles per hour with a scream of steam whistle and a brutal thud of sound that carried as far as Sunsmoke Desert.

It was grisly to watch, yet three keen watchers were grinning now as what was left of two big healthy mules was hurled into the sky, raining blood and guts and dismembered limbs upon the tracks. The Midnight Express was not equipped with a cowcatcher, as Strabo had learned when laying his plans. The hindquarters of a mule and a wagon-load of hardwood went under the engine and jolted the spinning wheels off the tracks.

Engine, tender and the pay-car with windows showing gaping faces staring out rocketed into the air, leaping over but not quite clearing the tumbling, rolling wreckage of the heavy wagon. The entire Red Horse Rock area shuddered as the spearing juggernaut hit and rolled three times across a hundred yards, crunching brush and snapping off full-grown trees with sounds like gunshots before sliding to a hissing halt in a ten-foot ditch.

Strabo led the way quickly for the broken payroll car. One whole side had been ripped out. Dead men lay scattered and two or three more were staggering dazedly about the wreckage. His gun emptied and their screaming ceased. Mailbags, cartons and crated goods had been flung every which way, many torn apart to reveal their contents.

But the wreckers weren't interested in chicken-feed tonight.

It was Sanger who eventually located the strong-box following a feverish search, and Hodge immediately ripped an engineer's axe from the rubble. But to Strabo went the honor of attacking the huge padlock. The chore took several minutes during which time the locomotive, lying on its side like a stricken dinosaur, continued to whine and howl like it was about to explode any moment.

Eventually the padlock gave way and Strabo bent to snatch up fat wads of neatly packaged money. He hurled them aside and continued to rummage. If Barney Brown was the ultra careful old bastard he was reputed to be, nothing less than the strong-box would have suited his needs for the transport of his map, he reasoned.

Strabo was dripping sweat before his hand closed over a small metal box. It was unlocked. He snapped the lid open, and only a man who knew exactly what he was looking for would have found anything even half-way interesting about a foot-square strip of satin-soft deerhide ornamented with drawings and symbols which only a gold-hunter could readily identify.

A solitary tear of pure emotion ran down the outlaw's face as he held the trophy aloft for all to see — then went plunging for his horse.

They were galloping away when the loco boiler blew with a roar that any dinosaur would be proud of. They got as far as the fringe of desert where Strabo and the map of the Lost Dutchman abruptly vanished as though the earth had swallowed them whole.

The situation was analogous with the aphorism; the operation was a success but the patient died. In this case, the big trail job was a resounding success but four of the five responsible finished up broker than they'd ever been before.

Could any man ever forget an experience like that? Would he even want to?

★ ★ ★

Erskine stirred. The memories of that fateful episode were still too vivid for him, too bitter. It was Erskine who had naturally assumed the leader's role in the search in the desert for Strabo and his treasure, following one false trail after another.

Erskine rose, blinking. The outlaws were all half-asleep as they lay sprawled out on their bedrolls like victims of a cavalry charge.

'Get up!' he said.

They groaned. Somebody cursed. They glared up at him with hatred. He was impervious, immune.

'It's still two days' ride to Wolflock. We daren't coach or train it on account they've still got our faces starin' down from every post-office wall in Nebraska. That only leaves horsebackin', and so that's perzackly what we're gonna do.'

'Go to Wolflock?' a man said. 'What the pluperfect for, man?'

Erskine spat into the fire and eyed

each rebellious face in turn.

'I'm sayin' the *derrotero* has got to be still there in that hard-knuckle town someplace. Strabo woulda had the map on him when he croaked, and someone lighted onto it. The fact that we ain't heard even a whisper of nobody leadin' no party into the Thousand Canyons country only means that whoever got to be new owner of our *derrotero* is playin' his cards close to his chest. Waitin' for the dust to settle. Wonderin' if Strabo's pards might show up lookin' for the Dutchman's map. Some canny, patient bastard with a real cool head.'

He paused and glanced around. 'Anyone not followin'?'

Hodge and Doone shook their heads, but Slim Sanger had something to say.

'Phil,' he drawled, 'So far as any of us know, there ain't been one whisper about that lousy map since the train job, and I reckon it'd be one hell of a risk to go sniffin' round that wild town with its law and all, no matter what prize money we'd be lookin' for. I'm agin' it.'

Heads nodded. Erskine spat in the dust.

'In the desert when Strabo gave us the slip with the *derrotero*, we pressed him so close and hard we forced him to quit the wild country and go lookin' for someplace quiet to hide. So, he had to have had that map on him when he landed in Wolflock and wouldn't have had the cussed thing on him when he bit the dust. Anyone wanna argue with that?'

None did.

'He was a thorough bastard son of a whore!' Sanger said bitterly. 'But he sure ain't worth dyin' over now. Is he?'

'Sure reckon not,' Doone growled.

'You ain't got nothin' more than what you just said?' queried Hodge.

'No I ain't.' Erskine's expression changed dramatically. 'On your feet!'

They were not quick enough in response. Erskine stepped back a pace and rested a gnarled hand on gunbutt.

'I won't say it again. Git your hosses

and git mounted. We are ridin' to Wolflock!'

One by one they rose. They didn't like it that Erskine was king here by right of might. Soon they were riding away and out across the bleak prairies.

They might hate Erskine tonight, but it was nothing compared with the hatred they held for Strabo. The way they saw it now, if there was even a remote hope of recovering 'their' *derrotero*, they must take it.

They rode out in silence, the weary horses flaring their nostrils at the sharp air.

★ ★ ★

Wolflock's Boot Hill was not much of a hill at all, more of a lumpy knoll rising from the plateau out in back of the copper-smelter which had closed down some years back when the veins ran out.

Even so, due to its position, the

graveyard by day commanded a sweeping view into the south-west across low-lying ranches and farms reaching all the way out to the great jumble of rocks of the malpai.

The night-comers weren't interested in scenery as they moved amongst headstones, tombstones and new graves, searching for a man whose boot-heels were more significant than they appeared to be.

Turning to check an inscription, McCall accidentally brought the blade of the store-bought shovel against a stone angel with a clang that caused his partner to jump a foot.

'Judas Priest!' Hogan protested. 'Why don't you scare a man while you're at it.'

'Thought you weren't scared about any old cemetery?'

'I'm not scared. I just don't want you to wake the whole town and bring that longbones sheriff a-runnin' is all.'

'It's OK to be scared.'

'I'm not scared.'

'You keep sayin' that.'

They traded stares. Hogan had succeeded in at least half way convincing McCall that a dead man's unique boot-heels might throw up the longshot lead they were seeking.

The search resumed.

One by one they examined the markers of men killed in turpentine-plant accidents, lungers, gunmen, ancient pioneers of the county, the occasional lawmen, fallen women and dues paid members of the Pilgrim Teamsters Organization.

Genuine badmen and outlaws found resting places of lesser prominence hard by in the Strangers' Ground, where the night-comers read names like Off Wheeler and Near Wheeler, Quick Shot Bob and a horse-thief, lynched by a mob, who'd borne the proud name of Oscar Hugo Paradise.

But no Strabo.

Finally they located the spot where a citizen as recently deceased as the previous day had been lain to rest. There were two new graves dug out alongside — suggesting that death was enjoying a boom in Wolflock at the moment. Yet not one sign of a hellion who had been shot to ribbons here five days before.

By this it was two in the morning with low clouds scudding across the moon and a chill wind blowing off the Finn River.

After a long dejected moment they climbed wearily onto their horses and rode down into a town that looked as empty as a hooker's hope chest.

They came across a weary hostler who was able to reassure them that indeed the fees at the Liberty Hotel were indeed encouragingly modest.

In response to a query by McCall, he also informed them that Cole Strabo still had not yet been buried.

5

Grave Matters

'OK, pilgrim,' said the stranger with the black ten-gallon and one sleeve empty, 'we're just gonna ask you one more time. When?'

'When?' echoed the undertaker, still startled to find his parlor suddenly crowded by strangers who wore scars and guns like badges of honor. He smiled weakly. 'Oh, I take it that you are more friends of the late Mr Strabo?'

'Don't mess us about, Graveyard,' warned a scarface who looked as if he kept busy helping people into hospital. 'We've ordered the flowers and the coaches and Two Gun here has booked the town band to be ready at a moment's notice to give Cole the right sort of send-off. Yet all we're gettin' from your people is that the funeral time's gonna be 'advised'. We want it advised right now, croaker. That's why we come to see you personal.'

Tiny droplets of sweat showed on the undertaker's brow.

'Gentlemen, I appreciate the fact that many of the late Mr Strabo's admirers seem very eager to afford him a send-off worthy of his, um, status in the community — '

'Get on with it,' warned Benny from Columbus. 'When? And why the delay?'

'I'm not sure when, and I'm afraid you will have to ask the sheriff about the delay,' Jones replied. 'I'm afraid all details are in his hands.'

The man named Texas cursed and promptly led his party through to the chapel, where the deceased awaited interment, to view the remains.

The parlor had done a fine job on the Strabo remains in light of the fact that a ruthless sheriff and three nervous deputies had shot him into doll-rags.

Encased in a silk-lined oak coffin with flowers, the brains behind the train robbery looked almost serene in repose as six hard faces stared down at him.

Two Gun sniffed. 'I hate the smell of these joints.'

'They don't always smell this way,' commented Benny from Columbus with the air of an expert. 'How long's he been dead anyways?'

'Hey you, croaker,' called the towering Texan. 'You got our pard on ice here?'

'Sure they have,' insisted another, a scar-faced man in an ankle-length gray duster. 'They'd have to. But why ain't he under the ground? Seems to me they ain't treating Cole with proper respect, leavin' him lie like this all this time.'

'I hate undertakers,' Two Gun said ominously. 'I reckon we owe it to Strabo's memory to convince this guy we want the job done — say right here and now?'

Eternity disappeared fast.

He was rushing for the rear exit when he suddenly skidded to a halt. The sheriff was coming across the yard with all three deputies in tow.

'Got word something was brewing here,' Wal Craddock announced as a relieved Eternity gratefully retreated behind his desk. Emboldened now, he folded his arms and bent a reproving eye on six suddenly wary strangers.

'Well?' the sheriff snapped, hands on hips and standing tall.

Looks were exchanged, uncertainty reigned. The motley crew who'd come to Wolflock to conduct a time-honored Outlaw's Funeral, had already found the town sheriff to be both a major surprise and an enigma.

A couple had already tried to bluff the lawman and had been mauled in the process.

So they went to water now, and Craddock treated them with the contempt they deserved. Hustling them out before him, he barked, 'Hup two, three, four!' and so saw them off — a top sergeant manhandling a bunch of rookies.

Eternity Jones was as impressed as

anybody, but had more pressing matters on his mind as he cleared his throat to speak. He begged the lawman to give his approval for the funeral, but Craddock just shook his close-cropped black thatch.

'The buzzards are gathering, Mr Jones,' he declared. 'Just as I predicted they would. I'm still confident that while ever we delay the funeral there's a chance that someone will show up who knows something about the map and the gold.' He held up both hands as the other made to protest. 'No arguments!'

Eternity headed off to the Lucky Cuss to down a stiff shot, then headed for the Green Rooms.

Over recent months the undertaker had fallen into the habit of stopping by at the dime-a-dance joint and putting good money down just to talk with Anna Fran.

Yes, talk. Every man needed some woman who seemed to understand him, and for Eternity that woman was the spirited yet hardly attainable girl-woman with whom Strabo had spent his last night on earth.

Theirs was an honest friendship. Both dreamed of getting a slice of the Dutchman's gold, if not the entire kit and caboodle. Jones knew of her interest, and frankly confided his troubles at the parlor, while she in turn proffered her opinions about the mine and the map. The way things were going, neither looked like benefiting should any information on the gold-cache surface now.

'So, what would you do in my position, Anna Fran? About the funeral, I mean?'

'You're the undertaker. If I were you I'd go ahead and bury him and the hell with the sheriff.'

'I've never seen Craddock so iron-mouthed about anything.'

'No mystery about that. He hopes if he cracks this case they'll promote him and transfer him someplace important. He believes there's a plot to keep him here, and that could even be so.

'So, don't be intimidated by the sheriff, Jones. Just do what you think is right.'

Eternity smiled. He'd gotten what he'd come for — some sound advice and the opportunity to enjoy delightful company away from the stresses of the parlor.

When he got back he announced that they would bury Whit Bowen later that afternoon. Bowen was a worker who made his living dynamiting old pine-stumps and selling them to the turpentine plant. Just yesterday, Bowen's luck had run out when a plug went off five seconds too early, ensuring a closed coffin for the deceased.

With familiar activity surrounding him now, Eternity sat back behind his desk and treated himself to another drink. Things were moving and he was making them move. He was looking forward keenly to cleaner air around the Heavenly Rest.

★   ★   ★

Hogan was musing on the night ahead as he finished knotting his bandanna and glanced across at McCall, buckling

97

up his boots. He frowned. Mostly they only ever bothered to smarten up this way to draw the women or — as was mostly the case these days — a particular woman with blonde hair and blue eyes who danced at the Green Rooms. But that wasn't the case today. Today they wanted to be seen as solemn mourners.

Hogan practiced his serious look. McCall shouldered him aside to check out the fall of his buttoned-up jacket in the mirror. He carried a sneak gun in his hip pocket in case of emergencies. He satisfied himself that the piece didn't make a bulge. This was to be a peaceful occasion in a town that was quiet enough today despite the presence of maybe up to a dozen strangers come to attend the Outlaw Funeral, all of whom looked tolerably dangerous. The two would prefer to visit the funeral parlor unarmed but it was not worth the risk.

'OK,' Hogan said, 'let's go over the plan one last time.'

'We've got a plan?' joked McCall.

Hogan didn't smile. This was serious. The dead outlaw who was still the prime topic of conversation in Wolflock was lying in state at the town's undertaker's under close security, with the sheriff a regular visitor at the Heavenly Rest.

The partners felt they could have well done without the additional hazard of so many Strabo admirers cluttering up the place, but had no option.

This was a serious situation in view of what they were planning.

'We go visit,' Hogan stated. 'We check out the set-up. Then I distract whoever's around while you whip Cole's boots off of him and stick 'em under that loose-fittin' jacket. Then we stroll out.'

'Sounds easy when you say it quick.'

'Let's get to it.'

It was late afternoon when they hit the street, two respectable-looking young men sporting stiff celluloid collars and spit-and-polish boots. Day laborers from the turpentine plant were arriving in Front Street in lumbering wagons, hopping down eagerly to invade the saloons where the first early strains of guitar and piano-music came lightly on the evening air.

Matrons shopped, pretty girls swished by looking good enough to eat, old winos stumbled down side alleys seeking to avoid the eagle-eyes of tough young deputies or a long-jawed sheriff.

The partners passed a handsome, hard-jawed woman holding court on a store porch, aware that she was the sheriff's formidable wife. They had no trouble identifying two men lounging against the same saloon hitch rail chewing cigars and seeming to look in all directions at once. The pair were friends, enemies or admirers of the late Cole Strabo come to take part in the final ceremonial.

They crossed at an intersection after waiting for a railroad horse-tram toting passengers along to the depot to roll by. Hogan winked at a redhead on the tram who smiled back at McCall.

Half-way along the stretch of sturdy plankwalk out front of the general store, the crowd suddenly parted to reveal the tall figure of the sheriff coming directly towards them.

Hogan looked boyish, McCall smiled amiably. Wal Craddock was not taken in.

'What mischief are you two cooking up?' he demanded, blocking their path with wide-planted feet.

Mischief? Them?

They were convinced they looked like a pair of shipping clerks out taking the evening air at the end of a hard day at the desks. The sheriff's narrowed eyes and flaring nostrils suggested he saw them in a different light.

'Evening, Sheriff sir,' Hogan said respectfully.

'Nice and quiet . . . just the way we like it,' McCall supported, gazing around amiably.

The last time the lawman had braced them was following a rustling out at the

Ten Mile. They knew nothing about it, of course. The man seemed to take a personal dislike to anyone who was young and didn't work twelve hours a day at an honest job — the way folks did back in Boston, apparently.

Craddock went on to question them about their recent activities, and they lied plausibly and personably. He paused as a group of three men strolled by, puffing cheroots. Strangers to Wolflock. More mourners?

'Humph! As if a man doesn't have enough to do with that breed hanging around without two hell-raisers like you showing up to boot.'

'You got us wrong, Sheriff.' McCall was wearing his choirboy look. 'We ain't trouble. Have we ever given the sheriff trouble, Hogan?'

'Not as I recall — '

'Just a moment!' Craddock snapped his fingers. 'Now I get it. Strabo!'

'Huh?' they said in unison. And McCall added: 'What's a Strabo, Shurf?'

'I sense buzzards drawn by the smell of blood,' the lawman retorted. 'Every shifty character in the county is sniffing around here these days, wondering about that lousy treasure-map, dreaming of getting their grimy hands on . . .'

He broke off. A man driving a trap going by almost brushed a woman carrying a huge bag of wash. 'Damned fool!' Craddock barked, starting off. He paused for a parting shot. 'Just keep your noses clean, Hogan and McCall. And while you're at it, keep away from Miss Hellinger. She's far too good for the likes of you. Hey, you in the trap, wait up!'

'He'll likely hit that poor geezer with a week in the hoosegow,' Hogan growled, running a finger round his collar. Then he nodded. 'But at least we've got a notion why he's always comin' down on us now.'

'We do?'

'That about Anna Fran. What business is it of his if we see her or not?'

McCall just looked at him without

reply. Anna Fran was special to both of them. Maybe too special. They shrugged and continued on their way, making for the Heavenly Rest.

A short distance on they came upon a group of mourners of a different stamp from the flashy hardcases they'd seen, but mourners nonetheless. The wake for pine-stump dynamiter Whit Bowen was being held at a central block saloon where vast amounts of beer and liquor were being consumed by turpentine-plant workers and their women, adding to the congestion of what the partners belatedly realized was a booming, bustling Friday night in Wolflock.

Hogan sighed as they put the overcrowded saloon behind them.

'You know, I can remember when Friday nights were a lot simpler — livin' it up, lifting petticoats and getting into fights when it didn't matter if you won or lost.' He gestured. 'This is different.'

'If your memory's that keen then you'll also recall Friday nights looking around at a hundred or two hundred hard-luck losers, and realizin' you were just one of 'em,' was McCall's tart reply. 'Then one day you started to use your brain and decided you weren't goin' to go on being one of that good old Friday night booze-up-and-getting-nowhere brigade.'

Hogan side-stepped a free-wheeling drunk and tipped his hat to three giggling girls coming arm in arm along the walk.

'Damn right,' he said seriously. 'That was about the time we started thinking of the future and keeping a sharp eye open for the big chance that'd lift us up by our suspenders and see us get to be something.'

It was their big dream. Be something. Make something of themselves. Ride tall.

Then back to reality. They had less than ten bucks between them.

And as luck would have it, they found themselves passing the hotel on the far side of the street.

They stopped to stare longingly at the Plains Hotel, the largest and most impressive building in town. Fifty rooms, a desk clerk who dyed his hair, maids in frilly aprons, bell-hops, a *maitre d'*, suites up to twenty dollars a night.

On one memorably boozy night as the partners walked Anna Fran home from the Green Rooms, all three had stopped out front of the Plains and vowed they'd own it one day and double the tariffs overnight.

Sure, it had been just foolish talk and an impossible dream. But Hogan knew McCall secretly took it seriously, as did he. Once or twice when their luck was running and easy money seemed to be flowing their way, the impossible dream had appeared vaguely possible. Right now it appeared more distant than ever — unless . . .

'We're wasting time and we've got work to do,' Hogan snapped. He led the way on until they stood before the sober brown doorway of the funeral parlor.

They paused momentarily as though freshly aware of just how dangerous their scheme seemed in the cold hard light of reality. And nothing was more real than a funeral parlor.

'Smarm our way into Eternity Jones's parlor, outwit a few dumb attendants, plumb the secrets of a dead man's boots and with luck and cool nerve maybe go galloping off into the night with a letter, a drawing, or hopefully a map, that might lead us to the Dutchman's gold — and maybe go out of our heads throwing it in the air like confetti!'

They'd said it, agreed with it, knew now they must go through with it.

A black hearse with two plumed horses in the shafts stood before the undertaker's, dusty from the Bowen funeral.

They walked right on inside to the lobby where they were met by a long-faced attendant who, upon learning they were Strabo mourners, condescended to show them through to the chapel.

From the corner of their eyes they glimpsed the solemn figure of undertaker Jones placing something in a drawer of the huge black lobby desk, possibly the fee for the day's burial.

Removing their hats as they entered the discreetly lighted chapel room, they saw several caskets resting on polished rosewood trolleys, each with its own candles and flower rack.

The caskets were sealed, including one of handsome polished oakwood, which was almost surrounded by flowers. Silently the attendant tapped a gloved forefinger on a handwritten card resting on this casket, which read:

Coleman Henry Strabo
R.I.P.

The faces of Hogan and McCall looked sickly in the candlelight as they stared at one another.

They'd been told the casket would be open.

'What good is this?' McCall hissed at

the attendant. 'We came to say farewell to an old friend, not gape at a screwed-down lid.'

'Sorry, sir.'

'What good does that do?' Hogan demanded querulously. 'I demand to see the undertaker — '

He broke off as McCall gave him a nudge and jerked his head towards the door. A bunch of hardface strangers was entering to move towards another casket. Hogan glowered disapprovingly in their direction.

'Ease up,' whispered McCall. 'You'll get us thrown out if we make a ruckus.'

'Exactly,' sniffed the poker-faced attendant. 'Will there be anything else?'

'Much obliged, we'll be fine,' assured McCall. The man moved off to wait on the other party, leaving them alone with candles, flowers and a securely sealed oakwood coffin.

'They told us — open casket!' hissed Hogan.

'Well, it's nailed down. What now?'

Link Hogan sucked in a huge breath,

held it a long time, slowly let it hiss out between his teeth and was almost calm again.

Then, after what seemed a long time, he leaned close to McCall's ear and whispered calmly enough:

'Only one thing for it. We take the freaking coffin!'

6

Dead Man on the Run

Standing in the shrouded alleyway directly across Seminole Street from the Heavenly Rest funeral parlor, Hogan and McCall paid no attention to the passing parade as they considered a major challenge to their ambitions to get rich quick.

'It could be done,' McCall murmured, playing his gaze over the building and surrounds. 'I mean, it won't be easy on account Jones keeps the place well staffed even at night, and some of those attendants are pretty husky. But we still can do it . . . mebbe . . .'

'Let me ask you something, *amigo*.' Hogan sucked on a freshly lighted cigarette. 'Was it easy for Strabo when he set his sights on that there train?'

'No, but . . .'

'Sure it wasn't. Well, what he took on that night was a hundred times riskier than what we're considering.'

'You could be right ... ' McCall studied his partner. He needed to know something before agreeing to stick his neck out on an operation which, should it go wrong, could land them in deep, deep trouble in Sheriff Craddock's town. 'You really believe those boot-heels are goin' to pay off, man? I mean, as long-shots go, we've got to be backin' a hundred-to-one outsider.'

'It's in the boot-heels. It's got to be — '

'Now, what made me certain I'd find you boys here?'

They swung sharply to see the very feminine silhouette approaching through the gloom of the alley behind. She had approached silently in stylish, rose-colored shoes of finest leather. Dancer's shoes.

They were surprised yet remembered their manners. Hogan took off his hat and McCall groaned at the sight of creamy bosoms revealed by a low-cut dress, masses of golden hair and eyes that conjured up romantic nights, fiddle-music and moonlight.

'Oh, hi, Anna Fran.' Hogan tried hard to make it sound casual. 'Er . . . didn't expect to meet up with you in this old alleyway. Did we, McCall?'

'Reckon not.' McCall had recovered from his surprise. He frowned in concern. 'But the man's right about the alley, Anna Fran. You don't make a habit of wandering around this way at night, do you?'

She stepped lightly past them to gaze across the street before replying.

'Only on nights when I come down with a strong hunch that fellers who I thought were my extra good friends might be up to something that they should just know I'd like to be in on.'

They stared at her. It was no secret between them that both had fallen for the dancer right from day one. But they were also suspicious, as was their nature. Why had she come alone to this place at this time? They weren't buying the 'hunch' story for a moment.

Her laughter was velvet-soft in the gloom.

'Boys, if we're ever going to get to be rich and famous together in this crazy life, we have to learn to trust one another, and not . . . ' She paused to turn and faced them squarely, her manner serious now. 'And not leave anyone out in the cold when something big is afoot. Is that right or is it right? I'd like to know.'

It was a big moment. Sure, they'd often discussed their dreams and experiences, sharing confidences and making big plans which most likely would never see the light of day. They'd been sincere when they spoke of the three of them taking on the world, yet there was no way they'd have even thought of inviting her in on a deal such as they were now considering.

This was the riskiest damned thing they'd ever dreamed up, let alone considered putting into action. They were planning to take hair-raising risks to get their hands on a strip of deerhide which had already cost many lives and might well cost even more.

Surely she wouldn't even wish to grab that potential disaster by the tail?

'All right,' she said suddenly in the silence, turning to go. 'I can take a hint. I'm sorry I had the wrong notion about us. I won't bother you again.'

'Wait!'

Hogan's tone was urgent. He seized her by the arm and swung her to face him. 'Girl, it's not like you think. But ... but tell us ... what brought you here? What are you hintin' about what we're doin' here?'

Anna Fran jerked free of his grip, angry now, eyes glinting.

'You men are such dupes! You think you're so clever. Yet any female with half a brain can read you all like clear print.'

'Meaning?' McCall challenged.

'Meaning last night at the dance.' Anna Fran tossed her head. 'You were so busy fighting over me and showing off that you didn't think for a minute that I knew from the moment you walked in you were hatching something and holding out on me. Don't you realize I deal with men who are liars, deceitful, crooked and double-dealing every damned day of my life?'

She paused for breath. Neither man spoke. When she continued her tone was calmer but certainly no sweeter.

'Today I was watching you from the moment you left the Liberty. I saw you getting pushed around by Wal Craddock, then I watched you make your way here to the parlor — you stood out like beacons to someone who suspected what you were about.' She paused for effect, hands on flaring hips. 'Well? Have you found Barney's *derrotero* yet?'

They were stunned. How could any female be that smart? She had them at her mercy and neither man tried to deny her words. What was the point.

'How did you figure?' Hogan asked at last.

'All those endless questions you asked me about Strabo's visit the night he died. You were about as subtle as a stage wreck. I knew then you had something in mind, now I know what. And I'm still very, very disappointed. So?'

They traded looks and nodded. It was still too damned dangerous for a woman, they knew. But this was not simply *a* woman but *the* woman. And they didn't even need to discuss it to realize that whatever risk they might be facing it didn't begin to stack up against the risk of losing her, which seemed a strong possibility if they didn't come clean.

Hogan let McCall spin the whole story. Anna Fran appeared unfazed. Indeed she appeared to be suddenly animated as she clapped her hands.

'How exciting!' she said. 'Wouldn't it be wonderful if we could do it. We wouldn't be hurting anybody. The Dutchman's gold always belonged to whoever could find it. I'm sure he wouldn't begrudge us having it and using it to make a lot of people happy, especially ourselves. So, what do you want me to do?'

They stared dumbly at her for long moments. Hogan was sober as he replied:

'Anna Fran, this isn't any game or — '

'What do you want me to do, Link Hogan?'

He shrugged and capitulated.

'OK, you're on good terms with Eternity. You could try and get him to close up shop for the night and take as many of his staff with him as you can talk him into.' He grinned reassuringly. 'Be nice to the old buzzard, but not too nice.'

'Men!' she laughed and was gone in a moment leaving them frowning after her.

'You don't think that old . . . '

'Nah. He's way too old.'

'He's rich.'

'You're right. You can get most

118

anythin' you want if you've got money.'

'Damn right you can. So let's get back to tonight and see if we can't get rich ourselves.'

Hogan broke off to draw his bandanna up over his face, signalled to McCall to do likewise. His voice was muffled when he spoke.

'I'm with you all the way. Now first check out that side drive and those wrought-iron gates . . . '

★   ★   ★

Cold sweat dripped off McCall's jaw as he casually trailed the hand-led horses drawing the hearse round the side of the parlor and up to the scrolled-iron gate leading to the yard in back. There were people everywhere this time of night and it was hard to keep in the shadows, dawdling along behind the sort of rig that would naturally attract attention anytime, day or night.

The attendant leading the horse

halted to unlock the gate. He then led the rig through with a crouching McCall on the blind side of the carriage. Keys grated, the gates were locked and McCall heard the keyring jingle into a pocket before the rig rolled on again.

It was a sizable yard with horse stalls and two sheds for wagons and hearses. Ground lamps gave off discreet illumination. Everything about this place was discreet and in good taste except himself and Hogan.

He shook his head.

Hogan thought of himself as an ideas man, he knew. But McCall reckoned he was more like a man with maybe too much imagination and reckless enough to try just about anything. Trouble was, he expected a partner to be crazy enough to go along with him.

The rig halted again. They'd reached a wagon shed. Out came the keys again and the attendant fiddled the padlock. Eternity Jones certainly believed in keeping all his possessions snug and secure.

McCall slipped a gun from the waistband of his pants. He came up behind the man as quiet as a falling feather and laid him out with one quick chop to back of the head.

He glimpsed a dim figure across the yard in back of the parlor as he grabbed the unconscious man beneath the armpits. He dragged him off into the shadows.

'Hey, what you doin' over there?' a voice called.

McCall averted his masked face and replied with something unintelligible, pocketed the keys and took a horse by the headstall, turning the hearse away from the shed.

The man was coming towards him as he started across the yard, swinging his arms officiously.

'I said what are you about? Hey, who are you anyway? And . . . and what are you wearin' masks for?'

'Sleep tight,' McCall muttered, and

sprang forward to belt the man off his feet with Samuel Colt's finest invention.

It went swiftly from there — getting the second man out of sight then pelting back across the yard to unlock the gates. He was breathing hard as he dashed back to the hearse and horses, and led them right up to the double rear doors of the parlor where muted lamplight spilled through stained-glass windows.

'We're loco!' he panted, tying the horses to the hitch rail and dashing sweat from his eyes. 'Why'd I agree to go along with it anyway?' And the answer popped up instantly: 'Because you didn't have a better idea, McCall. So quit griping and get on with it. Good advice, McCall, real solid.'

Now where was Hogan and Strabo's corpse?

It was just as well he didn't know right at that precise moment.

Link Hogan was a naturally strong man who was driven to a supreme effort tonight by ambition or greed — he wasn't sure which. He'd been able to slip Strabo's trolley from the chapel into the passageway leading to the rear without attracting attention, only to come face to face with a large young man in a leather apron emerging from the embalming room.

He reacted fast.

Using the casket-laden trolley as a weapon, he rammed it headlong into the startled attendant, slamming him onto his back. The trolley bucked from the impact and the casket slid forward off the trolley just as the dazed embalmer was trying to raise his head. The casket slammed his forehead, the back of his head slammed the floor and the the embalmer was all through for the night.

Across in the reception area, Eternity Jones and his casket carpenter stared up at one another in puzzlement across the undertaker's desk.

Was that a thud they'd heard?

Within the discreet and dignified

confines of the Heavenly Rest, the only sounds ever heard were just that — discreet and dignified. Never any bangs, thuds or crashes. Eternity was leading the way for the rear just as a feverish Hogan managed to get his casket loaded back onto the trolley again.

No time for fiddling with door-locks now; he could hear footsteps approaching fast.

Desperately Hogan got behind the trolley and charged full tilt at the double doors, which burst apart under the impact with screws and lock-pieces and slivers of splintering wood peppering a stunned McCall standing directly outside.

Desperation can invest people with abilities beyond the norm. As McCall reeled back down the steps clutching the casket to keep it on the trolley after half-demolishing the doors, Hogan reached him as he was about to tumble down the steps backwards. Lightning-fast, he grabbed the opposite end of the casket and whipped it round to face the rear doors of the hearse all in one fluid motion.

Regaining his balance, McCall heaved his end up onto one shoulder leaving his hands free to open the hearse doors. The casket rocketed in, the doors slammed shut behind it and two frantic figures were clambering up onto the padded seat as Eternity Jones and his night staff reached the shattered doors and started shouting like crazy.

With McCall plying the reins the two-horse span executed a tight semi-circle in the yard, which caused the hearse to teeter up on two wheels. Eventually the rig righted itself with a crash and Hogan laid a blacksnake whip across glistening hindquarters with a vicious crack of sound. The teamers broke into a startled run and went charging through the gateway, scattering pedestrians left and right as they swerved into the street.

Eternity Jones drew a pistol and began firing wildly into the sky. In twenty years in his profession he'd never had a body stolen before, and even now in his confusion and agitation he was clearly aware that this was about the worst possible corpse a man could afford to lose.

'After them!' he howled. His staffers rushed for the horses even if they mightn't fancy their chances of running down the cadaver-thieves. It appeared the body-snatchers were already making record time as they thundered headlong down Seminole Street making for the river, the bridge and the plains beyond.

★ ★ ★

One hour before the crash of Eternity Jones's gun jolted Wolflock from its Friday night normality, Sheriff Wal Craddock had arrived home for supper late, as usual, to find things pretty much the same as usual.

No wife present when he arrived to change shirt and socks and take a brief breather before returning to the office.

No freshly ironed shirt, nothing but a cold-beef sandwich on the kitchen table.

The sheriff's long face was dark and tight as he sat munching and staring at the cat.

Things were getting worse on the home front every day. And he knew why.

He'd ridden high with the marshal's office following the death of Strabo, but even such a coup hadn't led to his so-long delayed promotion. He'd had no option but to take a gamble on recovering the treasure map, but he knew it had failed, as did his wife.

She would make him pay for his failure. It didn't matter a damn to her that the town, the council and the county press regarded him as the best thing that had ever happened to this lousy town. She wanted to star at the county commissioner's annual ball and be recognized as the wife of the next chief marshal.

She was mercenary, shallow, ambitious and vain. And those were just her good points.

He half-grinned, then sobered as he sank his teeth into a chunk of cold, leathery meat.

Nobody in town understood why he was tolerating outlaws in town or why he kept insisting the undertaker delay the dead badman's interment. Certainly he kept the reason close to his chest. Yet you'd think the Wolflock man in the street would figure it out for himself that Sheriff Wal Craddock had to be playing some crafty game to be acting in such an un-Craddock-like way.

It made the sheriff feel sick to his stomach each time he strode along Front and encountered killers and thieves. But he could put up with them in the slowly fading hope that their presence might pay off in a lead on the money.

With sudden impatience, the sheriff jumped to his feet and reached for his hat. He went to the wall mirror. Every fortnight he had his bristling black thatch ruthlessly cut back by the

Mexican barber at Blades. It made his ears stick out. He liked the look. He didn't believe a peace officer should look like a tailor's dummy or a gunslinger wearing a badge. He jammed his hat on his head and set his jaw before turning to the framed photograph on the wall. The picture depicted his superior, the chief marshal, standing before his imposing headquarters on the streets of the county capital.

Chief Marshal Clay looked much the way he did, tall, spare of build, wang and rawhide tough.

They were very similar apart from the fact that the marshal was climbing up the ladder while the sheriff remained frozen in Wolflock.

He blanked his mind on that one, concentrated instead on mapping out his patrol route to the undertaker's. Eternity kept pressing him about Strabo and Craddock was at last ready to give in. His scheme had come to nothing. They might as well bury the outlaw tomorrow, after which he would boot the badmen out of town so fast it would make their heads spin.

Trudging from one street to another, the sheriff of Wolflock was lost in his private bitterness until the sudden thunder of guns erupted away in the direction of the funeral parlor.

★   ★   ★

Brick Hodge robbed the wash-line while his partners watched from the nearby brush. The householder was a worker at the turpentine plant, and by the time the outlaws reached the edge of town all were togged out in rough coveralls, which along with several days' growth of whiskers and tugged-down hats should afford them the anonymity they sought.

Even so they were not taking any chances.

Ever since the Strabo gang was identified as the men responsible for the robbery of the Midnight Express, posters depicting Strabo, Erskine, Hodge, Sanger and Doone had ornamented the walls and tree-trunks from Omaha to the Wyoming border.

They passed such a postered crab-apple tree *en route* to the abandoned farmhouse on the north side of town which would be their base.

Doone was selected by Erskine to infiltrate the town and get the lie of the land. The youngster with the barn-door shoulders and bushy black beard resembled his wanted dodger depiction less than did any of the others. Also, Doone was teak-tough and enterprising. The job Erskine charged him with was initially to find out if there had been any developments concerning the map since Strabo's death. If he proved able to do this without exposing himself to the risk of discovery, he would also check up on whatever the law was doing about the case. If there was time and opportunity after that, he was to go see that dancing blonde Strabo had always been talking about, see if she knew anything — anything at all. They

131

were getting desperate.

Enjoying the responsibility, Doone rode into town on his travel-stained horse and soon knew all about the delayed burial, the presence of big-time badmen in town, even stopped by at the Green Rooms to catch a breathtaking glimpse of Anna Fran who appeared to be anything but in mourning for Strabo.

He looked for but found no sign of the outlaw contingent reported to be in town. There was a solid reason for their absence. Under the chairmanship of an illicit slave-trader known simply as Tex, Strabo's peers were holding a secret and serious meeting behind closed doors at the East Sage Hotel tonight.

★   ★   ★

It was a sight to scare a snake — nine notorious outlaws from all over West Nebraska gathered together in one smoke-filled room beneath a shaded drop-light. Hunched, slumped, tensed

132

up or outwardly relaxed around a green-baize-covered billiard-table with carved legs almost as thick as Big Tex's biceps, they were listening as Darky Costello explored the reasons behind his mounting suspicions about life in general in Wolflock, from the visiting criminal's point of view.

'There's somethin' mighty fishy goin' on here, boys.' Costello was not an eloquent man but could usually tell how many beans made five. 'That proddy lawdog, the long delay in shovellin' Cole under. I smell somethin' and it ain't the fish I had for supper.'

Heads nodded, voices murmured in agreement.

These men who had assembled here were anything but *compadres* of an outlaw brotherhood. As Strabo had been, they were bloody individualists each exclusively out for Number One. True, some had been motivated to come to Wolflock to enjoy a genuine slap-up Outlaw's Funeral and a reunion with old associates, but nobody here tonight was deceiving anybody.

The prime reason they'd come was to be on hand should something surface about the map and the mine. It hadn't, and Tex had summoned them together to compare notes in the hope of discovering whether any individual might have caught a whiff of anything at all which could justify their staying on much longer. They were busy men. They had rustlings, bank-robberies and killings to get back to. Time was money.

The outcome of a half-hour's discussion was negative and depressing. Although vaguely suspicious of several people ranging from the blonde dancer through to the undertaker, the sheriff with his repeated delays of the funerals, and a couple of likely-looking young hellers named Hogan and McCall, nothing had surfaced to suggest any of these had any knowledge of the missing *derrotero*.

It would appear that the hardcases' entire Wolflock operation was shaping up as a failure. The whereabouts of the treasure map was as deep a mystery as ever; it might well turn out that Strabo had taken it with him into eternity — some thought it was just like something that bastard would do.

The night seemed to weigh heavily on their shoulders as the gathering of Nebraska's worst began filing from the smoke-choked room, which stood but half a block from the funeral parlor.

It was something to see the alacrity with which they hit the floor and whipped out their guns when someone close by began shooting like crazy.

Moments later they were joining the stampede for Seminole Street where some fool was screaming that somebody had stolen a corpse.

7

Where Bullets Fly

Standing in a crouch behind the splash-board clutching the driving-reins, Cade McCall sent the hearse hurtling the length of Seminole Street with Hogan applying the leather to the wild-eyed teamers as terrified towners leapt from their path.

They hadn't wanted it to be like this.

The plan had been to overpower a couple of parlor staff discreetly, slip Strabo out back then drive off sedately in the hearse and with any luck clear town before anybody was any the wiser.

Instead, Wolflock burst into an ants' nest of frantic activity as they continued to churn their way riverwards, leaving chaos, confusion and outrage in their wake.

'The turn, the turn!' Hogan suddenly

bawled, gesticulating wildly.

They were already well into the corner which would lead them on towards the bridge, before a desperately straining McCall finally got the teamers to turn.

The back wheel caught a neat white picket-fence and churned it up like matchwood which sprayed the startled householders who'd emerged to see what all the racket was about.

A big black barking dog was the next victim of wild driving and reckless haste. Engulfed by pounding hoofs and spat out behind from spinning wheels, the dog managed to get to its feet only to be run over by a tall and grim-faced figure astride a gray horse firing a .45.

They stared back as window-glass in the hearse shattered with a musical tinkle.

The body-snatchers couldn't believe the sheriff could have reacted to the sounds of trouble, commandeered a horse and got to lead the chase in such a short space of time.

They did believe, however, that the sheriff was no slouch with a Colt, as bullets whistled close, the sound of the shots drowning out whatever it was he was bellowing after them. He called upon them to halt or die.

'Shoot!' McCall shouted as they stormed around another bend.

'We don't shoot lawmen!' Hogan sounded outraged.

'Not at him — just shoot your gun!'

Hogan obliged. Bullets slashed the road well ahead of the sheriff's racing horse and ricocheted overhead. Well in back of the badgeman was a mass of riders comprising a motley posse of parlor staff and plant workers supported by visiting badmen with scarred faces. Craddock fired back, the slug burning McCall's right wrist, causing him to lose his grip on the reins.

Out of control, the teamers took out another fence and went plunging across several vacant lots, then ploughed through a line of trees as the two men fought to stay aboard. It was dark out here beyond the lights but there was still light enough to catch the shimmer of rushing water dead ahead.

The Dee had been their destination, but the plan was to cross it by bridge.

Instead they hit with the impact of a train wreck, the mighty wall of white spray concealing the confused tangle of hearse, animals and high-flying men which struck, went under then bobbed to the surface again as the full strength of the river swept them downstream.

McCall could hear the fading sounds of the pursuit as he grabbed at a piece of wreckage only to have it snarl at him.

'Link?'

'Who else were you expectin'?'

'What a freakin' disaster.'

'Or a stroke of luck. That tinstar had us until we bolted into the brush, I reckon.'

They were boiling along beside the half-submerged hearse. It rolled and something bobbed to the surface; they recognized the casket.

They hugged it like shipwrecked

sailors clinging to a life-buoy as the rushing river carried them beneath the bridge and beyond.

* ⋆ ⋆ ⋆

By the first sickly gray light of morning they stared into the white and very dead face of a total stranger.

Their eyes met over the casket, which had been smashed open hours earlier when it and the two men desperately clinging to it had been slammed into a rocky shore some miles south of the bridge in the darkness.

Battered and bruised and surprised to find themselves still alive, Hogan and McCall had sought shelter until dawn, assuring one another that it had to be some kind of omen of good fortune that, despite the crash, fate had seen them hang on to Strabo's remains.

Only now to discover it was not the outlaw at all.

For a long, dull time they just sat there with daylight struggling through the clouds which hung low over rough, almost badlands country with rugged red clay cliffs and twisted low hills reaching away from the Finn.

They couldn't figure this one.

The corpse was in Strabo's oak casket; his name had been displayed upon it on a hand-printed card.

Eventually, stirring to check the dead man out, they discovered something deeply interesting. He'd plainly been a manual worker judging by the calloused hands. It was equally obvious he had not succumbed to either gunshot wounds or natural causes. There were broken bones and severe burning, with hair and eyebrows singed away. Hogan suddenly clicked his fingers.

'Got it! The dynamiter. What was his name . . . ?'

'Bowen.' McCall nodded. 'You're right, it's gotta be him. But why in hell was he in Strabo's casket?'

'Because the undertaker's a fool?'

'That shifty old bastard's no fool. He doesn't make mistakes. Sharp as a stiletto and . . . ' He paused, looking up sharply. 'And tryin' to spark Anna Fran . . . ? Mebbe on account he figured she might know something about the *derrotero*, you figure?'

Hogan jumped up and the rays of the rising sun hit his tattered figure.

'He could have thought that . . . her bein' with Strabo the night he was gunned down . . . ' He began pacing to and fro, the swollen river a growling backdrop. 'What sort of scam are we gettin' a whiff of here, man?'

He indicated the broken casket.

'Like you say, that undertaker ain't the kind to make mistakes. There's been a swap in coffins here, deliberate you can wager. We find this dynamiter in Strabo's coffin, and they sure enough buried someone yesterday. So who was in that casket they put in the ground?'

'Strabo?' McCall said.

'Looks like it. But why?'

'Simplest reason could be it was all on account he was goin' bad, mebbe? Seems he'd have had to be . . . all that

142

time and what with the heat and all . . . '

'Makes sense, I guess. It seemed all along that Craddock was the only one who wanted him kept above ground . . . can't figure why. So, this could just be a simple case of Eternity gettin' fed up with havin' an overdue body lyin' about the place. He'd be wantin' to go against the sheriff but not game to do it openly.' He stopped and spread his hands. 'So he gets the bright notion to switch coffins.'

'Sounds like. Hey, man, you don't reckon Anna Fran would have known about this switch, her and old Eternity bein' kinda friendly?'

Hogan was silent a moment. He was crazy about Anna Fran, knew how crazy she was about money and success — just like themselves. But unable to figure any reason why Eternity would confide in her about the matter, he shook the thought aside and concentrated on the reality.

Which was — they'd risked their

necks to snatch a corpse and it was the wrong one. What he was considering now would be messy and likely a little crazy. But the simple fact of the matter was that they still needed to get to the right casket, the right corpse and the right pair of high-heeled riding-boots of Spanish leather!

He said as much and now McCall jumped to his feet.

'We wouldn't dast dig him up . . . would we?'

'We'd be loco to try.'

'That doesn't answer my question.'

They stood staring at one another for a long moment's silence. Hunting the *derrotero* had seemed almost like a game, at first. A game with a huge reward should they get lucky. They were used to taking risks but had taken far more than ever before on this one. That didn't alter the fact that it was still out there someplace . . . the Lost Dutchman, the gold Barney Brown had discovered . . . their key to riches, good times, maybe even respectability.

But if they wanted to play the game out it would mean more risks. All good poker-players knew that the more often a man sat down to the table the greater the odds that he must eventually lose.

That was the sensible way to look at the situation, surely? Or were they beyond that point? They weren't crooks, but they were risk-takers. They shared harsh, neglected and impoverished backgrounds, which in their cases had led to one common goal in life; get successful no matter what the risks, and there sure enough were risks aplenty here. McCall cleared his throat.

'Hmm . . . we figure we're sure Strabo's in Boot Hill right now under this man's name — and still wearin' his boots.'

'Right. So?'

'Did your mom raise you to be a quitter? Mine didn't.'

Hogan half-grinned, then turned sober again.

'They'll be lookin' for us all over, you

understand? The law, those outlaws, Eternity . . . '

'Sure. But will they be lookin' for us at Boot Hill at midnight?'

'I doubt it. Feel like hiking?'

'Never felt like it more,' McCall replied. 'But first things first . . . '

They spent an hour putting the casket back together as best they might, then toted it back from the river and concealed it in a nest of rocks. They would make sure it was known where the unlucky stump-blaster lay, no matter what awaited them back in town. Just as they would ensure that Whit Bowen would eventually be taken back and laid properly to rest. They weren't exactly upstanding citizens, but were a long way short of the badasses that that long-nosed badgepacker considered them to be.

If it ever came their time to die young and violently, as Bowen had done, they'd like to believe somebody would show respect for the remains and not just leave them to rot under the open skies with only screech-owls to mourn for them.

* * *

Eternity Jones was uneasy when he glimpsed the tall figure of the sheriff through his stained-glass windows. Men had been returning dejectedly from the manhunt all morning, and although it seemed that Hogan and McCall had either escaped or drowned in the Finn, the undertaker didn't know what else may have been found.

'How does he look?' he asked an attendant by the window as the badgeman halted in thin sunlight to tamp tobacco into his pipe. The undertaker had a guilty conscience and feared it might have been discovered that he'd swapped bodies yesterday, thereby deceiving everybody in general including the lawman.

It was not a hanging offence. But Wal Craddock had been so obviously obsessed with his last-ditch scheme to keep Strabo 'on display' that there was no telling how he might react to this.

'Tuckered, I guess.'

That was no exaggeration. The sheriff had been in the saddle all night in charge of the hunt for the body-snatchers. He'd conducted the search with his customary thoroughness and authority as he could always be relied upon to do, yet had come up empty.

His mood was strangely negative. The entire Strabo affair had been grinding him down, yet he felt he'd been more than holding his own until those two young hellions had turned his town on its ear.

En route to the parlor he'd encountered groups of outlaws who'd demanded to know the reason for the ongoing delay of Strabo's funeral. The snatch of the body, the presence of criminals in his town — to no advantage to him now — everything felt it was going to hell in a hand-basket. He was doing all a lawman could, but his dream of a quiet, law-abiding town — and his promotion and repositioning — were suddenly looking more remote than ever.

It was a tired badgeman, maybe even a beaten one, who entered the parlor around noon to inform Jones that he was free to go ahead with the Strabo burial immediately. He supposed he could not rightly blame Hogan and McCall's loco stunt for his uncharacteristic depression, but he would blame them until he found a better excuse.

The sheriff was anything but good company and Eternity was almost giddy with relief by the time the man eventually quit his parlor. Plainly Craddock still didn't know he'd switched bodies. Now he could bury Bowen as Strabo and none would be any the wiser.

The whole town was buzzing by the time Craddock trudged back to the jailhouse an hour later.

The undertaker had spread the word and at last preparations were now being made for the long-delayed Outlaw's Funeral. Gang-bosses and master-forgers, train bandits and kidnappers, swindlers, hit-men, cattle-thieves and killers for hire appeared on the walks and in the bars in tailored broadcloth, patent-leather boots, boiled white shirts and knotted silk ties, the very air surrounding them thick with the fragrances of Cuban cigars and Scotch whisky.

They were going to show this hick town something today.

The town band was tuning up behind the fire station and all the girls from the Green Rooms, Maisie's, the Midnight Rambler and Josie's Chicken Ranch had been given the afternoon off duty to attend.

Wolflock had never witnessed an Outlaw's Funeral before. It grabbed the public's imagination and made the raw frontier town feel almost cosmopolitan and colorful, things it had never dreamed of being until Cole Strabo had put it on the map.

Craddock found his first deputy waiting for him on the jailhouse porch. The grapeshot of telegraph messages they'd fired off to various East Nebraska authorities and law bodies alerting them to the body-theft had already brought some reply wires, one of which the sheriff carried inside where he read it with his boots up on the desk.

From a marshal of slight acquaintance in Three Forks came the information that the men in question, Hogan and McCall, had once escaped lawful custody in the company of the late Cole Strabo. 'I was right about those two,' he growled. Then scowled. The damned marshal had added a footnote to the effect that Hogan and McCall had subsequently been cleared of the trivial charge against them, were regarded in his quarter as 'fine upstanding boys with tons of energy and ambition who'll likely make fine citizens one day — if they don't kill themselves beforehand.'

He screwed up the slip and hurled it away. He supposed running off with a corpse wasn't a hanging offence. But he'd give a lot to know what was behind that caper; he couldn't shake the notion that the whole affair must be somehow connected with that accursed map.

Or was he just getting obsessive?

With his men awaiting orders, the sheriff leaned back and massaged his jaw, watching the street. His thinking had been right all along, he consoled himself. His hanging onto Strabo's remains and delaying his funeral had succeeded in attracting badmen and others with an obvious interest in the map of the Lost Dutchman; he'd just been watching the wrong ones, was all. He should have been watching Hogan and McCall!

He grimaced. He knew he didn't really believe that. Hogan and McCall were really small-timers while he was hunting for big fish. Now he felt ready to give up on Strabo, the stolen *derrotero*, the Lost Dutchman and the whole damn thing. Today's funeral would spell *finito* to the sorry episode of Cole Strabo's death and he would be glad to see the end to it.

'Finished!' he told himself aloud,

getting up. Sooner or later he knew he would round up Hogan and McCall and at least the body had been recovered. He'd fine them or jug the pair for a couple of days, then offer them their freedom in exchange for their sworn-on-the-Bible promise they would never but never show their lousy youthful faces around his town again.

He growled some orders to the deputies, then stretched out in his chair, closed his eyes and settled down for a nap. He was not looking forward to the Outlaw's Funeral, but would surely enjoy booting all those scar-faces out of his town the moment it was over.

He might not be going to make his promotion and he might well really be the loser his wife envisioned him to be. But he would continue to keep Wolflock law-abiding and clean. It could simply be that this proud and dedicated lawman had at last come to recognize his limitations.

★   ★   ★

Strabo would have loved it.

Blaring trumpets, blatting trombones and the stirring rat-a-rat-tat of the kettle-drum lifted the spirits and had people swinging along beneath banners and balloons as they cheerfully followed the hearse and main party out along the road to Boot Hill.

It was the Heavenly Rest's second-best hearse; its best, having been hauled from the river five miles below the bridge that morning at first light, was now reposing in the wagon shop awaiting repairs.

But Eternity Jones was driving in his best black broadcloth, the landau directly in back of the hearse occupied by a crippled rustler from Dakota along with Anna Fran Hellinger who'd brought along some of her girlfriends from the Green Rooms for a little fresh air and excitement.

Behind the landau marched a contingent of men in tweed and broadcloth finery and hand-tooled boots which contrasted sharply with the scarred faces and brutal eyes that accurately advertised their violent profession. Big Tex and his henchmen might well have come to Wolflock in the avaricious hope of catching a whiff of a certain famous treasure map, but had stayed on to now enjoy one of those rare occasions when they were able to appear openly *en masse* and attract the sort of attention they could only otherwise expect when they were either hanged or got shot to dollrags by some posse.

The atmosphere was festive and nobody made any apologies for that. In his lifetime, Cole Strabo had attracted attention, infamy and ultimately success of a kind. But no affection. There wasn't a damp eye to be seen, yet it was still a swell occasion. And when they reached Boot Hill, Reverend Barnes mounted a dais and boozily delivered a eulogy which none too subtly suggested that although Strabo might well be burning in hellfire right at that moment, those present might still stand a slim chance of making it through the

Pearly Gates, providing they mended their sinful ways. He was good-naturedly applauded.

The atmosphere turned boisterous and jovial as the mourners returned to the central block and hit the saloons in force, and their appraisal of the big day was virtually unanimous. A badman was gone, and a good time was had by all. Perhaps now Wolflock could settle down and get back to normal. Perhaps.

8

Night Train

The snorting locomotive hauling twenty-one cars of farming equipment up the long gradient towards Red Horse Rock suddenly became visible behind the wash of the searching headlamp which illuminated scrubby trees and jackpines, coarse oak and cedar.

Crewmen stared out as they passed the spot where the Midnight Express *en route* to Fort Cromwell had been derailed earlier in the summer. The wreckage had been removed but there were still great gaping wounds visible in the red earth to testify to the violence which had erupted here when the Strabo gang struck and brought a train to destruction.

The engineer jerked on his cord to blow a long mournful whistle as tribute to the crewmen and others who'd perished that fateful night.

It was a ghostly sound and lonesome, carrying far out from the tracks over the arid lands west . . . all the way to the fringes of the desert where the tracks of the guilty and those who pursued them had long since blown away.

The exact spot where Cole Strabo had ditched his henchmen and galloped off through the cedars and sycamores that night lay some ten miles west, close by War God Hill, unmarked and largely undisturbed ever since.

Up to the very moment when he'd actually held Barney Brown's intricately worked *derrotero* in his hands amidst the tangled wreckage of the derailed train, Strabo had boasted a reputation as a ruthless but tolerably loyal breed of leader.

Not any more.

The killer had changed for ever from the moment the deerhide key to the Lost Dutchman mine rested in his hands. Confronted with the real possibility of great riches, he'd realized he didn't plan to share up with anybody. So, at the very first opportunity, he'd simply drifted away from the others into the darkness and set out to open up a big lead on the bunch when they came after him, as he knew they must.

But shrewd Erskine had witnessed the dramatic change overtaking Strabo right from his moment of triumph, was keeping a close watch for that reason. With the result that when Strabo finally made his break, he quickly found himself with four angry hellions galloping on his heels.

The outcome of the pursuit was that, instead of skirting round the fringes of Sunsmoke as he'd planned, Strabo found himself forced to flee directly into the desert, simply to save his hide. But they were enraged and vengeful men riding in his dust, and despite his every desperate effort he found it impossible to shake them off.

For Strabo the ride became a nightmare; for those behind him a raging mission of revenge.

The running man eventually entered a vast sweep of sandy waste a bare mile ahead of his pursuers. His mount was slowing badly while Erskine continued to drive the men on ruthlessly, gaining every mile. All too soon Strabo found himself facing up to the fact that he might have to make a stand and fight to the finish. Not for a single moment did he even consider leaving the map behind for them and thereby escaping with his life.

Suddenly sand stung his face. Within minutes the Sunsmoke was swept by the blinding nightmare of a desert sandstorm from which the lone rider eventually emerged an hour later, totally lost but very much alive — and totally alone.

The gang was still searching the desert for him, half-dead from heat, thirst and exhaustion days later, when Strabo mounted the stairs of the Green Rooms in Wolflock to dance in Anna Fran's perfumed arms.

* ★ *

The hush of a July night lay over Wolflock but it was anything but quiet and restful atop the only high ground in town, the place they called Boot Hill.

The diggers were about three feet down by this time. The soil was loosely packed, as the burial had only taken place the previous day. Even so it was heavy work for men more accustomed to riding horses, playing cards for money and working their brains rather than their muscles in their eternal search for success and riches. Hogan was blowing hard and McCall had stripped to the waist as they wielded shovels under a blazing moon.

'My old man was a gravedigger,' Hogan panted as he paused to take a break.

'No he wasn't. He was a buffalo-hunter on the High Plains.'

'He was? So he was.'

McCall straightened and dragged his forearm across his face, mopping up sweat.

'Why do you have to bullshit all the time?' he demanded testily.

'Maybe because it's what I do best.'

'You can be damned digging ain't what you do best.'

'Don't go gettin' crochety on me, *amigo*. Just because we're wanted by the law, could get jumped up here any minute, ain't even sure if this box is gonna hold Strabo or not — or if his lousy boot-heels have got anythin' in 'em but sand or sawdust — don't start grouching and . . . '

At that moment part of the growing pile of dirt they were building alongside the plot headstoned 'Whit Bowen RIP' gave way and slid back into the hole, covering their boots.

Hogan began kicking at the big clods, fuming and cussing. McCall seized his arm and shook him.

'Get a hold of yourself, dude.'

'Dude?' Hogan cocked his fists. Both were groggy from exhaustion and jittery with tension. 'That tears it. C'mon, pilgrim, let's have it out here and now.

You reckon I'm wrong about the boot-heels, you blame me for snatching the wrong corpse and you got the dumb notion that Anna Fran likes you better than me — '

'Anna Fran?' McCall broke in, genuinely surprised. 'How did she get into this?'

'Yeah . . . ' Hogan panted, slowly lowering his fists and looking puzzled. 'How?'

'You in love with her? I mean . . . really?'

'Dunno. You?'

'Dunno.' McCall half-grinned. 'Know what I reckon we should do instead of fighting?'

'What?'

'Dig.'

* * *

Eternity paused in the gloom to examine the card on a casket. He moved on. It was a habit of the undertaker to wander about the parlor at night from his bachelor quarters in

163

back, but he'd never been as restless as during this long week, for any number of reasons.

He'd never been obliged to keep a body as long as he had the outlaw's, nor had he ever been tempted to defy Sheriff Wal Craddock as he'd done when he swapped corpses in order to get Strabo finally into the ground. His reason for taking that daring step had been love, or whatever passed for love in his dried-up little soul.

Anna Fran had been to see him that day. Their relationship was honest. She wanted his money and he wanted her body. But today the subject of where they were heading, if anywhere, had been totally forgotten in the aftermath of the body-snatching episode, which became their sole topic of conversation.

Eternity was fearful that it might somehow be discovered that it was actually Bowen in Strabo's casket. Sharp-thinking Anna Fran was now totally convinced that Hogan's and McCall's recent hell-raising actions had to be linked with a certain priceless map etched into a piece of deerhide. This possibility kept her tossing and turning nights in her big brass four-poster, thinking of the Paris gowns she could buy, the lovers she could take and the shrivelled-up old undertakers she could afford to dump if only Strabo had admired her enough to leave her his *derrotero* in his will.

There'd been a time when she felt she was genuinely in love with both Hogan and McCall. But cynical now, she wasn't including either in her dreams or plans for the future any longer.

'They knew something, they acted on it, and they didn't confide in me,' she had stated bitterly, dabbing at her eyes with a square of silk. 'Men are all the same. They say they love you, but show them a dollar bill and they forget your name.'

'They told you they loved you? Those bums?'

'Not in so many words. But a girl can always tell.'

'Seems to me that mostly what any woman tells you is a whole mess of lies,' said a disillusioned Eternity, watching a tear roll down the girl's cheek. If she liked those two well enough to weep over them, surely he was crazy to hold out any hope for his own prospects any longer?

He was amazed at how quickly he'd recovered now. It would have been a nightmare trying to keep a stunner like her all to himself anyway, he reasoned, with all those young bucks hanging around his door.

He found himself wondering again whether Clara might not be more his cup of tea. Clara was the sheriff's testy wife, and Eternity had had his randy old eye on her also for some time, all the while quaking in his boots for fear Craddock might ever suspect.

Leaning on a casket, he massaged his jaw and thrust women completely from his mind. At the moment, a far more absorbing question was still the one he'd first asked himself as he'd watched a pair of fools roaring away down the street in a hearse containing a casket with Strabo's name on it. Why? If that pair believed the body might hold the clue to the map half the county was looking for, they were in for a big disappointment.

He'd searched for that damned thing until his eyes dropped out. There was nothing there.

★ ★ ★

Sheriff Wal Craddock relaxed in his jailhouse chair with windows opened to the night, allowing a cooling breeze to flow through as he nursed a mug of freshly brewed coffee and considered his pinboard on the wall. The item he'd cut out and tacked up came from the front page of today's *Wolflock Progress* newspaper, an eye-grabbing headline:

GHOULS STEAL CORPSE
LAW FAILS TO FIND STRABO BODY!

Nothing like a failed twelve-hour manhunt followed up by that sort of editorial overkill to make a dedicated lawman wonder why he hadn't followed his father's advice and gone into realty!

His pipe was smoking, his gimlet eye was like a buttonhook attached to another document, this one a blue telegraph slip from the county capital. It was short and tetchy. Just like her. It read: GOT IT. BE BACK TO PACK. This charmer was from Mrs Craddock who had gone off to apply for a position as the representative of the Ladies' Guild on a special review board on women's rights associated with the Territorial Legislature.

She had warned him she would move out and carve out a career for herself if he continued to 'slide down the promotional ladder'.

Craddock's lean frame sank deeper into his chair as he found himself actually smiling. Maybe he was a little punch-drunk from adversity and bad news, he reflected. Maybe he should be worrying, but right now he felt beyond that. He was drifting, and it wasn't a bad place to be . . .

Absorbed in his reflections, he failed to notice either Doone leaving the central block, or the rancher entering it.

The heavy-shouldered young outlaw was heading back out to the gang's hideout north of town to report his failure to uncover anything on the body-snatching, or from his brief visit with Anna Fran at the Green Rooms, who obviously knew nothing about any treasure chart.

On the strength of this, Doone figured that Erskine would decide to up stakes and ride off and forget all about the Dutchman's gold. Either that or he might go loco completely and decide to take this crummy town by the throat and shake it until it delivered something about Strabo and the *derrotero* and a pair of twisters named Hogan and McCall.

In the aftermath of the daring snatch of Strabo's body, Erskine had realized that the names of McCall and Hogan rang a distant bell. They'd been in trouble with Strabo once. Strabo had told the bunch the story of his escape from a prison van with two 'losers' named Hogan and McCall.

Doone intended telling Erskine he believed that Hogan and McCall stealing Strabo's body plainly had to be connected with the map and the gold. But would Erskine be able to figure out why, even if that was the case? And would it matter even if he did? Those two crazies were gone and the long-bones sheriff had given up the chase. He sighed. Life on the dodge seemed to be getting so difficult these days that a man might have to quit and take honest work. And pigs might fly.

Pigs were very much in the thoughts of rancher Dog Daley as his battered ranch wagon creaked along Front in the middle of the night beneath a blazing full moon.

He had a sow about to litter at his place down along the Finn and by rights he should be out there. Would be but for what the dogs had found.

Dog Daley was a little man with a swag belly who smelt of dog and at times genuinely resembled one with his hairy face, beady eyes and pink, lolling tongue.

Tonight as usual he was accompanied by his closest friends, Sump Gravy, Miss Blue Head, Tiger, Spot, Foxhunter, Old Wolf, Morganza and Heeler.

Miss Blue Head could trail a fox further than any critter could run and never lose the scent. It was this talent that had caused her to go ferreting around amongst the river rocks in the late afternoon, and then set up such a barking racket that Dog just had to go along to investigate. Thus he discovered the corpse in the casket.

Deeper than ever in midnight gloom, Craddock heard the dogs and ignored them, heard the wagon draw up right outside and slid even lower in his cane-bottom chair. He didn't want to see anybody. The hell with them! This was the sheriff's night to brood and he was determined to do the job properly.

Dog proved just as determined to see him, and Craddock was ordering the man to hell and gone when the rancher somehow managed to make the words 'corpse' and 'casket' heard above his harsh voice.

Craddock was out the door like a shot. The dogs set up a wild barking as he approached the wagon. He silenced them with an authoritative curse, then jerked the broken and battered casket onto the tailboard.

It was a corpse right enough. Dead as mutton. But it was not Strabo but rather Whit Bowen. But how could such a thing be?

He could think of but one man who should know the answer. He had better know!

9

It's Only Money

Anna Fran shook her head slowly as she waited for the coffee to come to the boil in the little galley in back of the funeral parlor's reception room.

Her mood was blue tonight, uncharacteristically so.

She'd expected to find the undertaker still awake when she'd set out from the Green Rooms. She was restless and sleepless as she was so often at such times when the moon raged across the night sky and she fell prey to all the old yearnings and insecurities that had driven her all her life.

She knew she was always welcome at the Heavenly Rest, and tonight she needed to think seriously about her future, which, if she were simply to say yes, could see her become Mrs Eternity Jones.

No more wild nights or dancing parties if she agreed to become Mrs Eternity. No more dreams of hitting the jackpot and living a heady life of pleasure, excitement and uncertainty such as, until recently, she'd shared with swashbuckling Hogan and McCall.

Her former friends and lovers!

Anna Fran's face shadowed as she studied the coffee-pot. She still believed — irrationally she supposed — that Strabo might have intended to cut her in on his fortune from the Dutchman, had he survived. Too bad about that. Which brought her back to Hogan and McCall. To her they'd always represented the wildness of youth and adventure; she'd fed on their high hopes and unlikely dreams. But more than that, she cared for them deeply — or had done until they had betrayed her and cut loose. She'd considered them all three to be kindred spirits, was certain both really loved her even if they might not fully realize it themselves yet.

The pair had shown intense interest in Strabo after his death, and Anna Fran considered it kind of cute that they could imagine for a moment that she didn't latch onto what was really on their ambitious minds.

The map.

Even so, she'd hoped and truly believed, that should they ever unearth the lost *derrotero* they would surely cut her in as she certainly would them were their positions reversed.

That all seemed like just big talk and buffalo-dust now.

The partners had snatched Strabo's body and galloped off with it without even a so-long. God knew what they intended to do with it. But it had to be linked with the map and the Dutchman; no other explanation made sense. This realization had hit hard, leaving her disillusioned and where she was at that moment — driven actually to consider seriously the one rock-solid option she had of escaping from the

racy but uncertain lifestyle she followed, and embracing the straight life.

With the undertaker.

The coffee was ready. She was taking
down cups when there was a sudden
clatter and voices from the parlor. She
identified the hard-edged nasal tones of
Sheriff Craddock and Eternity's clacky
voice.

She was tempted to go on through to
see what all the fuss was about. Instead,
on impulse, she chose to take up a
position in the passageway and listen,
after distinctly hearing her possible
husband protest in a whiny tone: 'It was
an honest mistake, Sheriff. I thought I
buried the outlaw first and Bowen
second. But as it was, it was the other
way round.'

Unaware of listening ears, the towering sheriff grabbed the undertaker by
the lapels and began shaking him, not
accepting his explanation for a minute.

'Sheriff Craddock, this is assault!'

'No it's not, sir. This is assault!'

With the words, Craddock drew back

a big-knuckled fist. The lawman was most likely bluffing but the undertaker couldn't take the chance.

Once he'd begun, Jones's words came spilling out in a torrent, and the threatening fist slowly lowered. The undertaker held nothing back now that he'd gone this far. He confessed that he'd wanted Strabo out of his premises and under the ground in the hope that — with all that distraction and high drama finally behind her — Anna Fran would prove far more likely to settle down and give his marriage proposal serious consideration.

The sheriff was startled. 'You and her?' He was aghast at the thought. But he reminded himself he had bigger things on his mind. Such as the body mix-up.

Ageing visibly by the moment, Jones leaned on his desk and spoke straight:

'Right now as we speak, Sheriff, Strabo's remains are lying quiet and undisturbed beneath Bowen's marker at Boot Hill. And if the pine-stump dynamiter's body has been recovered then there's no real harm done. Don't you agree?'

But Craddock wore a strange expression now as he let the little man man go and stood tugging his earlobe.

'Just a moment,' he said at last, speaking so softly that the listening Anna Fran had to strain her ears to hear. 'Those two hellers stole that casket thinking it contained Strabo. The only sensible explanation for that which I can come up with is that they must have had some solid reason to believe there's something in the casket that could help them get their hands on the *derrotero*, which we all know Strabo had in his possession. They knew Strabo once, would know his habits and weaknesses, if he had any. Yessir, damnit, the *derrotero* had got to be the only reason they came here and started sniffing around . . . '

He paused, snapping his fingers, gaunt features suddenly animated.

'Don't you see? They didn't get what

they wanted. So what would they do after they found out they'd disinterred the wrong goddamn man?'

'Why . . . figured out there had to be a mix-up 'twixt Strabo's body and Bowen's, I guess,' Eternity hazarded.

Craddock's wild stare alarmed the undertaker as he rushed to a side window. With one jerk he ripped the shades aside to stare up towards the rising bulk of the bluff on which Boot Hill stood.

'Figured exactly that!' he repeated, turning slowly back to the room. 'And then figured that whatever it is they want so bad might be still up there with Strabo. Right?'

'You mean you suspect that pair would dast come back here and try . . . and try . . . ?'

Eternity was searching for the words when he realized he was talking to himself. He rushed out front to see the sheriff running back towards the jailhouse. Eternity looked up towards the cemetery, shook his head and went back inside. He called to Anna Fran, only to discover she also was gone, leaving the side door gaping open.

Amazing! he thought shakily, heading for the liquor cabinet. That long-ago day when he'd first taken up the undertaking profession, he'd never anticipated it might ever prove to be so exciting.

★ ★ ★

'Here, hand me that boot,' McCall panted. 'You are all thumbs, man.'

'I've got it, I've got it!' Hogan insisted. And he did. The heel of the boot that had been unceremoniously ripped off the corpse's right leg clicked and twisted in his grip, and probing fingers found the tightly folded piece of soft material within.

Slowly, almost reverently, he unfolded the deer-skin. It was a breathless moment as, still crouched in the grave, McCall snapped a vesta into life on his thumb-nail and the light fell full upon Barney

Brown's intricately designed and lettered *derrotero* with its illustrations and the notations which began with the words:

> *One hundred paces north by northeast of saddle-shaped out-cropping, then twenty-five paces due west . . .*

There were tears in their eyes. The night seemed suddenly to have taken on a cathedral hush about them. It was a sublime moment. They had parlayed everything they knew about Strabo and his attack upon the train and subsequent flight from the robbery site into the desert, into a reason to take up the outlaw's scent. It had been an undertaking fraught with peril and uncertainty which surely would have ended in failure, disaster, or both — but for Hogan's long-shot hunch about Strabo's boots. They had taken further hair-raising risks and damn near got themselves killed along the way, despite the fact that, deep down and secretly, both men had expected the whole operation to prove yet another failure in the ambitious but unremarkable careers of Hogan and McCall.

Until this moment.

What they were looking at wasn't simply just an outstanding example of the map-maker's art that might lead them to a king's ransom. It was a long-overdue vindication of their faith in their ability to pull off the Big One, some day.

They almost managed to bury themselves alive, so frantically did they then begin to claw their way out of the yawning grave. They dislodged half a ton of earth on top of themselves before a sweating McCall eventually clawed his way free and extended a hand to his partner.

McCall had Hogan half-way out when, from the corner of his eye he glimpsed a pair of boots planted on the loose soil just a few feet off to the right.

He cursed in alarm and released his grip on Hogan, who swore even louder as he slid back into the pit. McCall clawed for his .45 as he twisted violently to face the new danger. His jaw sagged in disbelief as he gaped up at the imposing figure of Anna Fran dressed in riding-pants and denim jacket with hands on flaring hips. She surveyed them calmly and coldly with the moonlight forming a halo about her golden head.

'Hey, sweetheart,' McCall grinned stiffly, uncoiling to his full height. 'Er, look, baby . . . '

'Forget the buffalo-dust, you double-dealers. That's the map to the mine, isn't it?'

'Mine, Anna Fran?' Hogan panted, clawing his way out unaided and trying unsuccessfully to stuff the deerhide into his shirt front. 'What mine?'

Her face turned to stone.

'Craddock will be up here any minute with his deputies and probably a whole posse.' She cut him off brusquely. 'Do you want me to start in screaming and bring him that much quicker? I will if you don't level and count me in. You have ten seconds.'

The partners whirled to look down upon the town. Sure enough, there was activity visible down on Front by the jailhouse. They traded one swift look then turned back to the woman. If ever there was a moment for lightning decisions it was now, and they proved up to the occasion. The horses they had stolen from a Finn River farmer were tethered nearby to a pine shadowing the Strangers' Ground. The mount Anna Fran had borrowed from the parlor stood at the cemetery gate. The moon blazed down, the game was afoot and the occasion demanded, and got, a decision quickly made and acted upon.

'OK,' Hogan said soberly. 'But before we move one yard, you've gotta believe one thing, honey. We weren't cutting you out of anything.' He gestured. 'We knew we were taking one big risk coming up here tonight, knew if someone about the sheriff's size caught us at it we could wind up like Strabo.'

'The man's tellin' the simple truth, girl,' insisted McCall, as serious as she'd ever seen him. 'We're the Musketeers, remember? You're in on this here caper, sure. But you'd be crazy to think of ridin' with us. Ain't that so, Hogan?'

'If we go we go together,' she snapped. And turned to her horse.

All three were up and riding within moments, with Hogan leading the swift way west.

When Wal Craddock sighted a drift of hoof-lifted dust ghosting away from the uneven crest of Boot Hill, he immediately began shooting and shouting to get his deputies into their saddles and using their spurs. The racket aroused the whole town. But only four hard-bitten strangers astride big grain-fed horses saw any reason to saddle up and follow the hunters and the hunted out along the cottonwood trail that ran due west.

★　★　★

The east arm of Sunsmoke Desert was a waterless waste dotted sporadically with a genus of cactus which could store water and another great rooted brush which was able to reach deep into the earth for what little moisture there was to be found, and survived on very little of it.

Underfoot, where the three stood by their mounts in the panting heat, lay not soil or sand along this ridge line they followed, but rather rock split into cubes by the heat, none of it smoothed or water-rounded at the corners.

Little tufts of sad, dry grass grew between the stones, grass that had sprouted bravely from one single rain only to die in a moment, as all things died here.

It was a day and an hour where no breath of wind blew, and tobacco smoke hung in the dead air causing one of the played-out horses to snort and rattle its head-harness, the small sounds quickly swallowed up by the vast silences.

'Drink?' McCall murmured, proffering Anna Fran his canteen.

'We can't afford to drink any more until we hit the spring,' Hogan said sharply.

'It's less than an hour away,' countered McCall. 'Go ahead. Drink.'

Hogan swore softly as water trickled down the woman's throat. Here they were, poised on the very brink of what might prove to be the adventure of their lives, with pursuit a long way off and possibly lost, yet there was increasing tension between them.

Both men turned to take a thoughtful look at the reason behind this.

Associations could develop fast at such extreme times, when people were thrown together in a dangerous situation, with the promise of vast rewards at trail's end. Experience was compacted and highlighted until it now felt as though the three had spent a year in one another's company exclusively, not just some thirty-six hours.

Anna Fran was the catalyst. Suddenly it was not just Hogan and McCall, but rather Hogan and McCall plus a woman who could make risking life and limb to grab at a possible king's ransom in yellow gold seem like the most sensible thing imaginable.

It was exciting in a way, their friendly rivalry sharpened by circumstance. But such a thing could also prove dangerous, something Anna Fran sensed, even if they might be unaware of it.

She'd seen riches, or even the promise of them, turn good friends against one another. Right at that moment, with their objective quite close now, she could sense the growing tension.

'How far now?' she asked, her voice calming and strong. She was focused on the gold, refusing to allow romance or rivalry to intrude. But it was easier for her. She had always thought Hogan thrillingly handsome and McCall was the sort of man a woman naturally felt she could lean on. She had two choices while they only had one.

The answer to the question she'd just asked was — not far.

A lone eagle sailing high above the

desert watched the tiny specks of the three riders moving on northeastwards across the predator's own kingdom of sand and stone towards the canyon country. Until its attention was diverted by movement far to the north where a massive canyon sliced the flatlands apart and a series of skinny stone buttes marched away into infinity.

Closer still, to the east, drifted another moving cloud of hoof-lifted dust raised by horsemen following the trail of the first party, which had just passed below the eagle's lofty summit.

With limited knowledge of the Sunsmoke or canyon country, the Wolflock lawmen had no option but to cling tenaciously to the trail of Hogan and McCall.

The situation was very different for the the third group of gunpackers now veering north-east away from the borders to the canyon country, riding the west flank of a black stone ravine towards the ugly, time-scarred prominence of War God Hill.

Erskine's hellions knew the north region intimately. They had veered away northward from Craddock's party shortly after quitting Wolflock, certain by that time that their quarry was making for the desert and the flanking Thousand Canyons region. For that was the area, lying between War God Hill and the steel tracks of the railroad, where they had ridden themselves into the ground the night of the train job when Strabo gave them the slip and vanished with the map to the Dutchman.

The double-dealing son of a bitch!

Big Erskine deeply regretted that others had had the pleasure of blasting Strabo into hell. But the anger was far behind him. Ever since that fateful night, himself, Hodge, Sanger and Doone had focused solely on the hope that somehow, somewhere that chunk of deerhide would fall into their hands and lead them to the gold at the end of the rainbow.

They were convinced that the law's headlong pursuit of the grave-robbers simply had to be related to Strabo and the map. But there was no way they intended going down there to get lost in the Thousand Canyons — which every citizen in the county knew concealed the secret of the Dutchman's gold. They were too smart for that, or at least Erskine was. He figured that, no matter what came to pass in the canyons today, with the law in pursuit of those flash bastards, Hogan and McCall, the only safe way out of the danger country would have to be to the north — where their horses were now churning up the dust. And when they came — whoever might come — they would find them waiting.

A tiny dust cloud visible far away across to the south told the outlaws their quarry — or quarries — were making impressive time, and there was urgency now in the way four grim-jawed men flogged flagging horses along a brutal back trail threading through the raddled hills. They were certain that the cloud of dust pin-pointed the posse's position, but now the Hogan party appeared to have vanished.

Desert-wise Hodge insisted that the trio appeared to have been swallowed up by the Thousand Canyons area, known to the desert-wise as a hell on earth.

The outlaws kept glancing at one another as steel-shod hoofs struck sparks from brittle rock, while above, that dot in the sky floated serenely under a murderous sun, remote, aloof, untouchable. Each man knew that the expression he saw on the other faces was stamped upon his own. Ever since the stunning triumph in plundering the Midnight Express it had been a long list of betrayals heaped upon disappointments until they had degenerated from a methodically dangerous bunch of badmen into embittered losers searching for solace in liquor and recrimination.

But a pair of smart-ass nobodies had torched the flame of hope again, and

Lou Erskine and company were now prepared to ride until their horses dropped, to drink cactus juice and take on anything the wild country might throw up at them if that was what it took to succeed in what might prove to be their last slender chance to grab at the Dutchman's mystical gold.

The eagle floating above saw it all and was untouched. It knew neither greed nor ambition, therefore such factors couldn't threaten its existence. But down below on the sun-stricken surface of the parched skin of Nebraska, the danger was great.

* * *

McCall's brass pocket-compass had never come in handier.

'Two hundred paces due north!' he yelled, holding the instrument in his left hand and gesticulating with the right. 'Straighten up, damnit. Veer left . . . left!'

His figure rippling in the heat haze,

Link Hogan kept veering left until McCall signalled he was on line. McCall was counting out loud: 'One-eighty-one, one eighty two . . . '

It was mid-afternoon and the westering sun threw black pockets of deep shadow into the countless canyon crevices of the geological nightmare land. In remote ages past the sprawling region had been subject to thousands, perhaps millions of years of a great flood age which gouged everything that was loose out of the landscape, in the process creating canyon after canyon beyond counting.

The first Westerners had dubbed it the Thousand Canyons country, and for once were on the conservative side. Likely the canyons numbered several thousands, one barely distinguishable from another, a bewildering and intimidating maze generally avoided even by the Shoshone, Comanche and nomadic Pawnee.

The Dutchman had discovered a seam here and, though nobody ever saw it, everyone knew there had to be a map or maps. A gopher would be lucky to find its way back if it ventured more than two or three canyons from home base here.

Nobody knew how long Barney Brown had hunted for the mine out here. But he'd eventually found it, had died for it and now three others were prepared to risk the same fate — unless of course the *derrotero* delivered them quickly to the site — and unless wild Indians, gold-hunters or the law got them first.

Hogan paused to sleeve sweat off his gleaming face. Some distance away the horses stood spraddle-legged, slowly recovering from the brutal journey. A surprisingly cool-looking Anna Fran stood leaning gracefully against an outcropping nearby with one booted foot resting against the stone behind her.

She appeared composed while McCall was all preoccupation with map and compass. Hogan now walked with a hint of a swagger as he continued on to reach Barney's 'two hundred paces due north' mark.

It was like a game the partners played in which the objective was to see who could act the more nonchalant while each inwardly fretted at the desperately valuable time it was taking to follow Barney's careful directions.

Behind their impassive masks pulses were racing and eyes continually swivelled westwards, the direction from which trouble would appear. When, not if. There had been dust constantly on their back-trail, sticking there like a fat yellow burr, ever since Modoc County. How many pursuers were involved with Craddock and what their composition might be they could only guess. But the danger was real and the threat of it had driven them to push labouring mounts to their limits in order to stretch their lead. They'd had no choice, not knowing how long the search for the mine might take. You couldn't hurry this end of the operation for fear of error. They went about their work deliberately, yet not for a moment was any of them free of the image of hoofs surging through yellow sand . . . steel guns glinting in the sun . . .

At last Hogan reached his mark. McCall immediately jogged out to join him. They spent another precious minute arguing over the next setting.

Sixty paces west by south-west.

With McCall juggling the compass and packing their grave-digging shovels, they paced it out together to arrive at yet another junction which appeared not one whit different from any of the myriad just like it across the brutal landscape.

They again studied the *derrotero* together until something caught the corner of Hogan's eye up along the rim of the dominant canyon. After a frowning moment, he realized that what he could see was an empty canvas sack, which contrasted sharply with the red dirt beneath.

Frowning, he moved forward several

paces to come suddenly upon clear sign left by unshod pony hoofs which came in from a side canyon and led off towards the high bank where the sack lay.

He indicated to McCall to follow and trotted forward. Up close, he realized the entire sloping wall was extensively marked by human and animal tracks which the weather hadn't yet erased, leading both to and from the rim.

'Shoshone!' McCall muttered, picking up a scrap of painted eagle-feather. Next moment they were clawing their way up the canyon wall to reach the crest, surged over the rim, propped on a dime.

The Lost Dutchman lay before them. Or, more accurately, what was left of it.

They knew it had to be the mine in an instant, what it could only be. From where they stood they could see the mine shaft leading down into shadows and deep darkness. The entire surface area was littered by timber planking, canvas sacks, camping-equipment, tools and human detritus. The shaft had collapsed upon itself; everything was broken and scattered.

It was easy to picture how either the Dutchman or Barney Brown had crafted a shaft cover from the planking, then covered it with dirt to form a camouflage that only sheer luck — or maybe the eagle-eye of an Indian — might see through.

'I don't believe it!' McCall gasped bitterly. 'Hidden out here all those years — just waiting to be found — then red guts chance on to it just before we show up!'

'Guess that's how it happened, sure enough.' Hogan grunted as he hunkered down to finger the sign. He gazed around. 'Could be the Indians had no good reason to come along this canyon for all those years. But when they eventually did . . . well, one set of their eyes is worth a hundred of ours. Let's take a look below.'

By the time they were through searching the deep work-hole and the collapsed and cobwebbed shaft some time later, Anna Fran had rejoined them. There was no easy way to tell her the gold was gone, they just let her see for herself. The subterranean shaft-head was littered with tracks, trash and empty sacks. Even a town girl's eyes could see the indentations where the miner had stacked sack upon heavy sack against a vertical earth wall. The scavengers had left nothing but piles of loose earth and slabs of broken timber amongst the rusted machinery, had obviously gathered up every last nugget before vanishing off into the Sunsmoke.

So it was ended.

The daring, the danger, the sky-high hopes that had fuelled them every mile today, all brought to nothing. The plans they'd made to go into business together back at Wolflock, to quit taxi-dancing, chasing badmen or risking trouble with the law . . . how foolish all that seemed now. They'd even considered checking out the current asking price on the Plains Hotel when returned safely to Wolflock with their fortune.

You couldn't blame the Indians. The Shoshone had had more than enough experience with the gold-hungry white-eyes not to understand exactly what their find would mean to them. Guns, purchasing power, maybe even eventual independence.

It was coming on towards sundown before they could muster the will and energy to begin to climb out. Anna Fran went first, followed by Hogan with McCall reaching the ladder last. McCall was taking it the worst, which might have accounted for his slipping and falling heavily. He tumbled down the littered slope of the shaft, cursing like a muleskinner until he clawed at a sliding slope of loose rock and earth thrown up from the tunnel below to halt his fall. The entire slope came down over him and Hogan went plunging down after him. But a ton or more of material was no match for an angry McCall as he erupted free of the slide coated in gray sludge and elbowing at a rock that had struck him on the shoulder then wedged against his chest.

Then Hogan saw it was not a rock.

McCall realized the same thing simultaneously and they grabbed at it together and lifted it by its ends. It was a tightly packed canvas sack some twenty inches long with a six-inch diameter, and seemed to weigh a ton!

'My God!' Anna Fran gasped from above. 'Is that . . . is it . . . '

They were already certain what it was. But Hogan whipped his Bowie from his belt and slashed the canvas to make certain. Fat, egg-sized nuggets of yellow gold slid from the slit into their hands.

They were forced to sit down, staring from the sack to one another, then to the girl as she jumped excitedly down from the mouth to land in the soft earth surrounding them.

'My sainted mother, it is!' she gasped, snatching up a nugget and touching its smooth, rich weight against her cheek. Her eyes were like saucers as she focused on two dust-streaked faces. 'But how?'

'They missed one,' McCall said simply. 'There's empty whiskey bottles every place in this junk. The bucks likely got on the firewater when they realized what they'd found ... and somehow this one got overlooked. Either that or old Barney stashed it in the wall in case he came back one day and found he'd been robbed.'

'How much do you figure?' Hogan's voice seemed to echo in the shaft like a voice in a cathedral.

McCall tried to look professional as he hefted the sack.

'Thousands, that's for sure.'

'Are we talkin' grubstake?'

'Go figure!'

McCall looked boyishly excited as he rose on his knees and tossed him the sack. Hogan caught it with a grunt, hefted it.

'This is a big-time grubstake, *amigos,*

sure enough.' He reached out and threw an arm around Anna Fran's shoulders. 'Someone up there likes us. What's it matter if your cards don't win the main pot so long as you don't leave the game busted. What do you say, Anna Fran?'

But the girl didn't reply. Her horse was visible standing by the mouth of the claim where it had acted curious about the noise and excitement they'd been raising. But suddenly the animal faced away to stare off eastwards, both ears pointing sharply forward, its whole frame alert and suddenly tense.

'It sees something!' Anna Fran leap up and started up the ladder. 'I'll see if I can see what . . . '

Her words cut off as she reached open air. She took one look and went pale. 'They're coming across that mesquite hill. It's . . . it's the law!'

They were out, up and riding within a frantic half-minute. In that time the possemen had dropped from sight into the canyons. But Craddock would have no trouble following their sign; there'd been no time to blot their tracks. If they were to give the badgemen the slip, it could only be through cunning, craft and pure horse-speed.

They struck north.

This had always been their plan should success come their way in Thousand Canyons. South and east were too closely settled by dirt farmers living on the rim of the desert, while west lay the terrifying Sunsmoke itself. But to the north lay some fifty miles of stony hills gradually blending with the prairie country.

They had no way of knowing that Erskine was out there, any more than the outlaws were aware that Craddock, with his intimate knowledge of the region following the law's exhaustive search for the train-wreckers, had figured all along that should the three succeed in recovering the gold, north was the only logical run-out they could take.

Dust climbed the sky as three

hard-ridden horses pounded across shale, gravel and sun-withered grasses. To the east, possemen shaded red-rimmed eyes and orders were issued. While watchers of a more murderous breed saw it all and veered their mounts north-east away from the canyon country to follow dimly marked trails which would intersect that of three racing riders at a place named War God Hill.

10

War God Hill

Wal Craddock snatched the tattered canvas sack from a deputy's fingers. He stared at it with haggard eyes before returning his attention to the yawning shaft sunk in the canyon rim. Sweat streaked his face as he tugged hatbrim low against the probing sun.

'They did it!' he mouthed, half-triumphant, half-frustrated. They'd run the runners down to what was plainly the Lost Dutchman, which in itself was something to brag about. But the gold was plainly long gone, their horses were on their last legs, and there was no sure-fire way of knowing how much head start Hogan, McCall and Anna Fran had on them. He raised his eyes to follow the clear tracks of their quarry arrowing away towards the strange dark hills. He heaved a sigh, studied the blowing mounts a moment, then grunted: 'Well, what are we waiting for? Let's get on with it.'

Three deputies groaned in unison. They were young and fit yet the sheriff had run them into the ground. Sure, they were eager to bag their trio, especially now they realized they'd missed out on the Dutchman's cache. But they were not obsessed in the way the sheriff was. They were just peace officers doing a job while Craddock was a man driven by obsessions he could not even name but which were very real and raked him like a spur.

The deputies continued to protest even as they crawled into sweat-stained saddles. The sheriff was deaf to their complaints. Yet as his long-legged buckskin faltered beneath his weight as he swung up, Craddock knew the odds were against them. Their quarry had a head start in alien country and he was aware he mightn't have one damn thing to charge them with even if — as seemed quite certain judging by what he'd seen here — the gold had already gone long before they'd arrived.

But even with all the odds seemingly stacked against him, the lawman could only keep on.

So he led the pursuit across more unmapped territory with no knowledge of water-holes, trails or conditions, a boogered horse underneath him and a trio of played-out deputies on the point of rebellion trailing far behind.

But Craddock's jaw set harder with every mile, even though he was eventually forced to drop in back of his party to ensure no man tried to quit.

A long hard time later they heard the stutter of gunfire somewhere up in the shadowy hills beyond the canyon lands. In an instant, eager men who'd honestly believed they couldn't go another mile were kicking ahead and loosening their guns.

Wal Craddock permitted himself the luxury of one tight-lipped smile as he spurred after them. Gunfire was good.

It meant their party had encountered trouble of some kind — he would wager his badge on it.

* * *

A roll of guns crashed and echoed upwards and across the east face of War God Hill.

Anna Fran kept reloading the rifles while Hogan and McCall continued firing them. The first concerted volley they'd loosed after having being driven into this deep rock pan in the canyon by the outlaws, had accounted for one man and his horse. Since then, however, the battle on their part had been totally defensive as Lou Erskine expertly led his killers inexorably closer by making full use of the loose rock cover and giant brown boulders littering the savage gash of the canyon before them.

They'd found the outlaws waiting for them at Crow Canyon. Anticipating them. Erskine had identified himself and given the option: surrender or die. They still had the gold and their horses, but with no prospect of using them. The outlaws wanted to believe the party found the Dutchman, were prepared to kill to find out. The hellions had the advantage of numbers, terrain and most important of all, ammunition.

The defenders were running low and the situation was growing increasingly desperate as McCall pumped a round at a quick-darting figure before turning swiftly to Anna Fran for a reload.

Tousle-headed and dripping with sweat, he stared hard at her for a moment then abruptly dragged her roughly against him and crushed his mouth to hers. Maybe it was a crazy thing to do with death droning close, but somehow he couldn't resist; it could be his last kiss, his final breath. She seemed to understand as she returned his kiss with full passion, and a watching, smoke-darkened Hogan felt his heart lurch.

He knew damn well what was

happening here. Maybe rushing head-long towards the end of their footloose lives, he was ironically realizing he'd found the two things in life that had always eluded him, big money and the right woman. Seemed McCall had made the same exhilarating-tragic dis-covery in the same hour — if that kiss was anything to go by. And Hogan wondered: would God be sadistic enough to allow him this high moment of achievement and understanding, then snuff him out in the same hour?

The ricochet that came smoking off a boulder to drill a hole in the crown of his hat sounded like an emphatic 'Yes!' to him.

'OK, lover boy!' he yelled at McCall, bronzed face gleaming in the suffocat-ing heat. 'You gonna die smoochin' or fighting? Just let me know, will you?'

Instantly Anna Fran beckoned and McCall came running. All three embraced fiercely, and as Hogan's eyes met McCall's over her golden head, Hogan heard another door of revelation creak open. Cade had fallen also, and at the same time. After months of flirtation, high times, rivalry and treasure-hunting, the former friendship of all three had been tempered in the crucible of danger to evolve into something unique and close.

But all too late. How much irony could a man swallow in one dose?

A Big Fifty rifle thundered and all three ducked low. For this shot had not come from the swiftly encircling enemy but rather from the direction of the trail they'd followed into the canyon some twenty minutes earlier.

They looked up in total disbelief to see riders with glittering stars on their chests storming down the trail, Wal Craddock leading with a smoking rifle held at the port.

'What the Sam Hill is going on here?' the lawman bellowed, slowing his lathered cayuse. 'Anna Fran, I want you to get clear of those bums and take cover.' He raised his voice. 'As for you other men doing all the shooting up there, throw out your rifles and come out with your hands up. This is Sheriff Craddock of Wolflock speaking. I order you to surrender in the name of the — '

His voice was engulfed by a volley of fire and a deputy's horse went down, screaming and kicking. Craddock bellowed orders and his party vanished into a gully, only to reappear a minute later higher up, from which point they opened up, working on Erskine's party which suddenly found itself at a severe positional disadvantage.

Marvelling as gunfire stormed and the sky shrouded with gunpowder smoke, Hogan and McCall shook their heads in admiration. They'd always known Craddock was no man to mess with. He was proving it yet again, and they were deeply proud of the stiff-necked bastard!

For savage minutes the battle raged to and fro across the shale-splintered slopes of War God Hill, while from below Hogan and McCall repeatedly snatched freshly loaded rifles from Anna Fran's quick hands to blast away at each and every enemy move.

A man fell with a gurgling scream which was quickly swallowed up by a fresh crescendo of gunfire, snarling and vicious. For what seemed an eternity, yet which was in reality mere murderous minutes, the battle ebbed and surged as blood flowed like water and the tattered swirls of dusky gunsmoke thickened, partially blocking out the sun.

The two were startled when Craddock, whom they thought to be across with his men, suddenly shouted down to them from rock cover not a hundred yards upslope.

'They're making it tough so I'll give you a chance neither of you no-accounts deserve!' The sheriff paused, eyes lingering on Anna Fran. He ducked as a ricochet powdered a boulder crest close by. Now he gestured urgently. 'Get mounted and get that girl to hell and gone out of here. Well, what the tarnal are you waiting for?'

Hogan and McCall traded stares.

They hadn't expected this. Not from old iron-britches Craddock. They wanted to jump astride and ride like hell, yet didn't move. For deep down, they saw themselves as heroes. Were they too vain or stupid to do what they knew they should, and let this man out-hero them?

Then: 'Thank you and bless you, Sheriff Craddock!' Anna Fran's smoke-streaked face wore a smile as she slung a rifle over one shoulder and headed for the horses. She paused. 'Come along, you two ... ' She frowned in puzzlement when Hogan and McCall stood their ground, still wrestling with either their vanity or their consciences. Anna Fran stamped one small foot and swung the Winchester muzzle in their general direction. 'Now! Don't you realize this isn't one of those crazy games you're so fond of playing.'

That hurt, even if it might be half-way true. But then she half-smiled, which took some of the sting out of her words. Yet it remained crystal-clear that she wanted them to take up the sheriff's offer, and when they took a second look at one another, they realized that so did they.

The moment was cut short by a fresh volley of outlaw fire which came whistling and ricocheting through the cottonwoods.

They saluted the gaunt figure above and ran to the horses.

All three leapt swiftly astride and swung their nervous mounts away in time to glimpse Craddock's lean figure spring up and vanish upslope, running in a low crouch back towards the danger.

A short minute later three racing riders erupted from the wash travelling abreast at the gallop to go drumming away through the shards of talus that littered the base of War God Hill. Away from the gunsmoke and the killing until they gained the safety of a sheltering draw, where the sounds of battle were muffled and dim.

No bullets came searching them now, or later. For the enemy was in no position to concern themselves about anything but simple survival now, with Sanger lying bloodied and lifeless across a deadfall with three bullets in his chest and Doone nursing a bullet in the back, yet still dangerous. Only the iron Erskine remained unscathed, but proved too obsessive to take flight. Instead the raging killer elected to press the attack against two deputies in the gulch they'd chosen as their defensive position.

It was a fatal error of judgment as the outlaws soon sensed, when the sheriff, having taken off alone to flog his lathered horse up and around to the east flanks of the shrouded hill, suddenly loomed above and behind the killers' position afoot with his Big Henry barking like an angry giant.

From a stone bluff a mile distant, three motionless riders listened pale-faced to that rolling crash and roar which marked the final bloody minutes of what had once been the Strabo Gang. Now Hodge lay dead ten feet from where Erskine was choking on his own blood in a chuckwalla hole, leaving Doone alone without any course but to fight to the last against a man more remorselessly determined to stay alive than any of them.

'*Mucho gracias*, Sheriff . . . ' McCall murmured, with no way of knowing who lived or died. 'You mightn't make it home, but at least we got enough now to throw you the biggest wake party of all time.'

'No parties,' said Anna Fran, moving her horse alongside his and extending both hands. 'And, thank you, I'll take care of that now, Cade.'

'Huh?'

'Don't you see?' she said. 'We're all the same and just as foolish as one another, following a dream, looking for easy money in your case, or a rich husband in my own. Well, we tried for it and it nearly killed us. But we have survived and we have a little money and a whole lot more common sense now, and we're going to make the most of it.

The three of us.'

'Three of us?' queried Hogan. He liked to make the decisions but Anna Fran seemed determined. She also sounded like she was speaking pretty sound sense.

'Together,' she said with a smoky-eyed look filled with promise. And although Cade McCall wasn't sure just why he did it, he silently handed over the cash and watched her tuck it away in a saddlebag. He turned his head to see Hogan nodding approvingly.

'The three of us . . . together,' Anna Fran repeated. 'For always . . . now.'

Moments later the rim was empty and War God Hill Canyon was left to the victors and the dead.

★　★　★

Eternity Jones stood before the boarded-up windows of the Heavenly Rest Funeral Parlor, arms folded, chin sunken against his high, starched collar, the most mournful sight in a town which no longer boasted its own undertaker.

There was irony in the fact that the smartly dressed woman heading for the stage depot toting a valise should be the wife of Sheriff Craddock, the man who had personally shut Eternity down and cancelled his license on the grounds of unprofessional practice relating to the matter of the switched caskets.

The undertaker wanted desperately to confide in someone about his innocence, his evil misfortune, his foolish yearning for a girl one third his age and the harshness of the sheriff, her husband. But Clara Craddock, as usual, was in no mood to listen to his petty grievances when hers were so relatively huge.

'That man has had his last chance,' she snapped, glaring back along Front. 'Despite his extermination of the outlaws, and saving three so-called citizens, the marshal's office has again treated him with contempt. Commendations, a pay increase but not one word about a transfer or promotion.

Well, I've had enough at long last. I'm going, and for the last time. It was bad enough all these years when ... Are you listening, sir?'

He wasn't.

'He's closed me down, Mrs Craddock, and undertaking is all I know. What am I going to do?'

The woman stared at him with contempt, was striding off again when, in an uncharacteristic moment of concern, she paused and called back:

'News just reached the jailhouse. Cholera up at Rock Springs. A major breakout. Dying like flies.'

Eternity brightened. 'Cholera?' he said the way a miner might say: *Gold!* 'Ma'am, you've made my day.'

Mrs Craddock didn't respond before vanishing behind the dusty blue Concord and six. Eternity's eyes were swimming with excitement. Dying like flies, she'd said.

Then he yelled, 'Hold that stage!'

★ ★ ★

It seemed to the sheriff that this mid-afternoon hour was the first genuinely quiet moment he'd had following the drama and turmoil of recent events.

The shoot-out at War God Hill, his good lady calling it quits for which he sincerely hoped would be the last time, his failure to achieve transfer and promotion . . . things he'd done and other things he should have done . . .

Hogan and McCall surely headed that list. He supposed he should have charged them with something, still could if he wanted, seriously doubted he would bother.

The pair were now swaggering around town like conquering heroes. They'd broken no specific law in going in search of the Lost Dutchman, and finding it. Yet he still could have booked them for something, might well have done had not Anna Fran interceded on their behalf, or had he been less bitter about his failure to be properly recognized for his latest achievements.

He ground his teeth. Last night the marshal, down from the capital and taking too much to drink at yet another function honoring the sheriff, had let it slip that head office considered him the only officer in the county capable of holding Wolflock together.

Craddock had been told quite bluntly that he could expect high praise and pay increases in the future, but no transfers.

It was a huge compliment of sorts, he brooded. Head office knew what a troublesome region this was, sitting out here on the fringe of the deserts and Indian lands, and they were telling him that nobody else could handle the job.

Even so, he knew he should quit. He knew he could, but for the fact Wal Craddock never quit from anything.

He told himself he must stay on for one simple reason. He believed the place would just plain fall apart without a strong hand at the tiller.

He was sitting there on his lonesome when a deputy arrived back from patrol, wearing a strange look, or so the sheriff thought. In his usual gruff way he demanded to know what he wasn't being told, and the wary deputy advised that Hogan, McCall and Anna Fran Hellinger had just made an offer to buy the Plains Hotel, currently on the market at $8,000. The offer had been accepted. They'd paid cash.

The lawman sank deeper into his favorite chair. The way those three had been partying and parading round town ever since surviving Thousand Canyons and War God Hill, just as though they didn't have a care in the world, had already aroused his deepest suspicions.

Now he was certain. They'd found something out there in the canyons. It was the only thing that made sense. He doubted that between the three of them they might have been so lucky as to muster $80 legitimately, much less $8,000.

He felt intensely bitter yet hardly surprised. For in a striking and clear-cut way, that trio typified the town and the entire region, the 'morality' that existed here at the far side of noplace. They had no values here and he was a fool to believe that, in electing to stay on at the expense of his marriage and his self-respect he could ever change things one iota — he might as well at least be honest about that now.

These people would surely never change and things would never be any different. Not ever.

The sheriff raised his hand and ran his fingers through his black hair.

* * *

The sheriff raised his hand and ran his fingers through his gray hair.

He stirred and rose to take down his hat for the last time. His fingered his star and his gunbelt hung on the peg behind the door as he mused . . . where had all the years gone?

Late afternoon light lent a softer look

to Front Street as he stepped out and closed the door behind him for the last time. As suddenly he was plain Mr Wal Craddock, a stranger to himself.

He unpinned the badge and slipped it into his pants pocket — and it happened.

Within the space of just a few steps he felt himself overtaken by the strangest sensation he'd ever experienced as he walked the main street for the first time as an ex-lawman.

He paused by the steps to gaze about him. The entire town suddenly looked different, *was* different. No wild hellions galloped half-broken mustang ponies down the main street. Tumbledown honky-tonks had been replaced by a bank, department store and an attorneys' solid block of brick chambers. Everywhere his gaze fell it met neatness and order, the occasional well-dressed citizen . . . he could feel the peaceful quiet.

It was as though his five-pointed star had imprisoned him in a zone of resentment, distrust and blunted ambitions to such a degree that he'd been unable to realize that under his authority over the intervening years, Wolflock had grown up, had shaken off the yoke of its two-gun past and become a place where children could play in the streets or women walk abroad alone at night without fear.

It was almost like being reborn for him to walk a Front Street that looked mint-new to his eyes, aware he'd been blinkered and blinded all those years.

It was a stunning revelation, an epiphany for a badgeman.

Then he noticed something else, something that had nothing to do with the changes he was seeing, but with simple reality. For surely the unnatural quietness and absence of people on the street couldn't be part of his amazing revelation.

Where was everybody this afternoon? As though on cue, a man emerged from the refurbished and renovated Plains Hotel, a well-dressed man in his mid thirties who didn't wear a gun, just an easy smile. The sheriff scowled. Over the years they'd actually become friends, much to his surprise. He also had to concede that the three of them, Hogan, McCall and Anna Fran had somehow turned out to be model citizens and leaders in commerce and society. But today of all days he didn't want company of any shape or size.

★   ★   ★

'Hogan,' he grumped.

'The big day, eh, Sheriff? Come in and have a drink on the house.'

'Maybe another time . . . '

'Today.' Hogan sounded bossy. Then he added mysteriously, 'It's got to be on the day.'

He took him by the arm. Craddock tried to draw away but Hogan was too strong. Craddock swore as he was boosted through the front doors to enter the wide lobby where a hundred well-dressed men and women instantly turned and raised their glasses to chorus: 'Happy retirement, Sheriff Craddock!'

It took a lot to shake dour Wal Craddock, but the realization that every prominent citizen in his town had seemingly assembled in his honor without his having the slightest hint of warning, managed it.

Then he had a glass in his hand, they were singing the Nebraskan anthem, and next thing he knew the speeches had begun.

They overdid it, of course. The sheriff was embarrassed by what mayor, lodge president, pastor and even Anna Fran — still a vivid beauty — were saying to him and about him. Yet at the same time he was growing tinglingly aware that this might well be the proudest moment of his life. And the guiltiest. For how could he have been so wrong about this town and its people for so long?

It still wasn't over.

Anna Fran kissed him and gave

another little speech while McCall, losing his hair and looking prosperous, shook his hand and assured him he was far too young to retire.

Then Hogan got up on a chair like the show-off he still was, called for silence, and made the presentation.

'Well, you've heard everybody admit how deeply we all are in your debt, Sheriff. But if you think we're just going to sit back and let you drift away from this town you've built and pre-served, you've another think coming. Right, Anna Fran?'

'Correct, Link.' The woman smiled. Her gesture was all-encompassing. 'We all agree you're far too young to retire, no matter what the marshal's office says, Sheriff Wal. As you know, we're expanding into timber and cattle and desperately need someone of honesty and authority to run the hotel — at double the pittance you've always been paid.' She swung to the crowd. 'Who says he must accept?'

They cheered him to the echo and

a dazed Craddock needed McCall's strong supporting hand on his elbow as the man whispered:

'You could have nailed us on anything or nothing after the Thousand Canyons caper, Sheriff, but you were bigger than that. But you going easy on us that day told us we owed it to ourselves to grow up and start playing every game straight . . . *compre?*'

The crowd hollered for a speech, but the sheriff simply stared at Hogan, Anna Fran and McCall now ranged before him. It was almost painful for him to comprehend that what they were doing stemmed not from guilt but from their innate generosity of spirit and — even more difficult for a hard and solitary man to believe — out of affection and respect.

The last scales dropped from the sheriff's eyes and he saw clearly that they had never been bad, just simply different and unashamedly Western. And with that understanding came another. All those years he'd wanted

Wolflock to be Boston, had expected rough-riding cowmen to act like East Coast bankers, when all along they were simply being themselves, nothing more and nothing less.

With sudden strength Craddock climbed up onto the dais. He found his voice as he motioned for silence.

'My friends . . . ' He could not have said that before today. They waited for him to continue. He was not a man for speeches, emotion or even simple gratitude . . . or had not been. He knew, and they could sense, that he had become another man.

'My friends, I am grateful — more than you'll ever know. And, Hogan, McCall and you, Anna Fran, I'm proud and honored to accept your offer . . . '

His word-well was already running dry, yet somehow he managed to get out what was in him to say.

He stood very straight and raised his glass.

'Fellow citizens of Wolflock, join me in a toast to a place and time and way of life which I believe I've only really discovered today . . . the finest place on this earth. I give you — the true West!'

'The true West!' they chorused, and every glass was drained.

THE END